Ashton

Ravenwood Academy Book Two

Ashton

Copyright © 2024 by C L Easton

Cover Design: Black Pirate Book Cover

Publisher: Black Rose Publishing

Ebook ISBN: 978-1-998910-07-6

Paperback ISBN: 978-1-998910-08-3

Ravenwood Academy Book Two

C. L. EASTON

"There is no exquisite beauty
without some strangeness in the
proportion"
-Edgar Allan Poe

Author Note

Welcome back to Ravenwood Academy

The twists and turns will keep you on your toes.
Can you figure out who the stalker is?

Object Insertion, Dub-Con/Non-Con, Anal Play,
Alcohol and Drug Abuse, Mention of S.A, Stalker,
Torture, Murder, Parental Death,
Depression/Suicide Talk

Playlist

Lovely (Piano & Cello)- The Wong Janice, Benny Martin

Heart-Shaped Box- The Hipster Orchestra

Jealous Sea- MEG MYERS

Daylight- David Kushner

Dizzy- MISSIO

Paper Houses- Deb Never

King For A Day- Pierce The Veil

Sticks and Stones- Silent Theory

HEARTBEAT- Isabel LaRosa

Drugs- UPSHAL

SPIT IN MY FACE!- ThxSoMch

NIGHTSHIFT- MOTHICA

You're Somebody Else- flora cash

Her Eyes- Fame on Fire

Playlist

Drive- Deftones

4 Walls- Arden Jones

Granite- Sleep Token

The Magick- Witchz

After Dark- Mr.Kitty

Bang Bang Bang- Sohodolls

Pump It Louder- Tiesto, Black Eyes Peas

Lil' Red Riding Hood- Sam The Sham & The Pharaohs

Stalker's Tango- Autoheart

Suicidal Thoughts- Josh A

Fire Escape- Call Me Karizma

Work Song- Hozier

One

Ashton

Why are things in life so hard? One minute you are playing in the sandbox, and the next, you are sitting in your stupid Bio class pissed off because the kid you asked to finish your assignment didn't fuckin' do it, and now you're looking at getting kicked off the swim team for sure. Stupid fucking cunt.

I'm gonna beat the shit out of Archie.

I wait for Prescott to show up as the professor and coach discuss my grades. You swear I was failing every single class. It's one class. All I know is I'm hunting down Archie after this.

Prescott walks in, searching the room. His eyes land on me, the disappointment on his face is easy to read.

"Professor Normous, can you explain why I'm here?"

Norm-ass glares at me before turning to Prescott. "Yes, Ashton is failing, and we would like to discuss our options before we remove him from the swim team."

Prescott rubs his face. "I see. Have you discussed all the options before kicking him off the team? I don't know." He shrugs. "Get him a tutor? It's not that hard, Edward. I'm not sure why you had to drag me all the way down here when you could figure this out for yourself. You are the professor, after all, and you." He points to Coach. "Grow the fuck up. We all know you hate my sons being on the team. You haven't even tried to find out who tried drowning him. I should have you replaced."

Oh, snap. Take that, you cunt.

Norm-ass' face turns beet red. "Why should I tell him to get a tutor? He hasn't even applied himself. We're one month down, and he hasn't even passed one test or assignment. Whose idea was it to place him in this class, Prescott?" he spits out.

Prescott chuckles. "Well, his transcript shows he was excelling well in Grovedale, so either they were lying, or you're a shitty teacher. Which is it? Should I do a performance evaluation?"

Shit, here I thought Prescott didn't care about me like that. I watch as the coach weasels closer to the door.

"I wouldn't, Scott."

I think that's the first time I've heard the coach's first name.

"I have things to do. Obviously, this doesn't include me anymore. When he gets his shit figured out, let me know."

My eyes bug out of my head. "The he that you are referring to is standing here and had won you a gold fucking medal over the weekend. Dickhead."

"Ashton, that's enough," Prescott barked. "You help him pass, or you're both done. He stays on the team, and that's final." With that, he slams open the door and leaves.

"Well, you heard the man. I'm out until you figure your crap out." I salute the fuckers and leave.

Ace is waiting, leaning against the wall, spinning his smoke in his fingers. A quizzical brow arching above his left eye. "Well? What did numbnuts have to say?"

"I don't think they expected Prescott to go full Daddy mode on their ass. I stay on the team, and they have to do their jobs."

He chuckles. "Good. How hard is it to teach a bunch of twenty-something-year-old assholes?"

"Hard. Dickhead." I need a fuckin' joint.

The sun damn near blinds me when we walk out of the campus. I dig into my pocket, pulling out my joint and tucking it between my lips.

"Have you heard from her yet?" Flicking my lighter, I close my eyes, inhaling deeply.

"Not since she kicked us out Sunday." He rolls his eyes.

Someone is still slightly salty about getting kicked out of Jinx's place. I don't blame her. It freaked her the fuck out getting that text from Perv McGee. She wanted to meet him in the food court, but we all talked her out of it. There was no way in hell we were letting her go out there. Besides, how were we going to know who it was, and who's to say he would show up?

"If you want to see her so badly, she has music. Go visit her."

"I don't want to distract her, and I'm trying to do better here."

I bite back my laugh. "Sure ya are. Whatever you need to tell yourself. I gotta go find a nerd."

"Need help?"

"Nah, this will be easy."

"Fine, see you later."

I take off in search of one geek that's gonna shit his pants. It's easy to find him; luckily, Archie never leaves the café. That fuck is done for. Like last time, Archie is sitting at the same table typing away on his laptop.

I slam his laptop shut, causing him to damn near jump out of his seat. When his wild eyes land on me, he pales.

"I'm sure you remember me. Did you forget something? Fuckin' important?" I spit out.

I swipe his computer off the table, and it crashes to the floor.

"A-Ashton. I-I didn't forget. I swear." He looks around for help.

"No one is going to help you. I was almost kicked off the swim team because of you."

I lean in close, caging him in. I watch his Adam's apple bob up and down. That's right, be nervous.

"I'll get it finished today."

"Yeah, you will, or I'll be back." I push away from him, placing my two fingers at my eyes, then back to him in an I'm watching you motion.

He better pray to whoever he can that he finishes it on time because I am not sacrificing dick shit for this school. If I get canned from the swim team, what else is there for me here? I push my way through the lineup, getting a few glares and comments in return.

I head to my art class. If anything, splattering some shit colors onto a canvas should get me out of this angry mood. If only the teacher would let me paint what I want, things would go much smoother, and I would probably pass that class more easily. It could be worse—at least I'm not Ace.

The sight before me makes me want to die.

Ace is in the center of the class, standing on a small podium, posing like a douche. No one in their right mind sits on a bench, crossed-legged, resting their chin on their hand, except my brother.

I bite back my laugh, but the glare that Ace gives me, is the push I need. I burst into laughter, disturbing the entire class.

"That's enough, Ashton. Take your seat before I ask you to leave." The teacher sends deathly glares at me from her desk.

"Hey, you're the one that did this." I point back at my brother before taking my seat.

I catch Spencer grinning as I grab my paintbrush.

Fine, he's all right.

"I want you to draw our subject using expressionism. Tell me what you see and feel on your canvas."

Well. This is bullshit. I can tell you what I see. I grab a glob of black paint and paint Ace. He's lucky that I was blessed with the genes of being an artist. Only when I apply myself, but in this case, I think I'll pass and make him look like a donkey. Besides, the teacher did say to express yourself.

I want to see Jinx, but I feel the right thing to do is wait for her to come to me. I think I come off as a little intense and need to step back. Deep in the back of my mind, I should tell her what happened to me, but with what's happening with her, I don't want to add more shit to her plate, besides my problems aren't as significant as hers.

We need to work hard to find her pervy little stalker. The list Ace printed out hasn't been much help; who knew how many guys go to this school? And every class is different. It's a lot of cross-referencing, and it's not like we can call up the cell phone and strike up a conversation in class to see whose phone rings.

"Did you seriously paint me as a fuckin' donkey?" Ace grabs my painting off my easel.

I burst into laughter at the look on Ace's face. "Fuckin' rights I did. Explain to me how you landed in that position?"

"I was late one too many times," he growls.

"Ah, so you were punished. Lucky me then." I shoot him a huge smile.

He shoots me the middle finger along with a grim smile in return.

"Have you heard anything from Mad?"

"Just that he's at the music hall with Jinx. Maybe we can grab supper, drop by her place, and surprise her."

"Okay. Where the hell did my asshole brother go?" I stare at him in disbelief.

He rolls his eyes at me. "Give up. I'm trying an alternative path, remember? Grab your shit. Let's go."

An alternative path, my ass. I will give him until tomorrow, and the dickness is back. He doesn't have a nice bone in his body. He's only lying to himself, and it's not healthy. I don't need him taking it out on Jinx when he does crack.

"You go back, and I'll grab something to eat."

He points at my painting. "Fix that piece of shit."

Nah, I'm gonna frame it in the dorm room. I think it'll be perfect there. Or better yet, a birthday gift.

Once Ace leaves, I clean up the art room. Being the last one here gives me some alone time, which is horrible for remembering the past. My brain doesn't get the memo that we don't want to remember certain past events.

Especially one college house party memory.

I need to get out of here before I fall into a black hole that I won't be able to climb out of.

Two

Maddox

Things have been strange since Sunday. I wish I could put my finger on it, but it's hard. Jinx hasn't been talkative with us, and she's been pushing us away. If she thinks space is what's needed, she's fuckin' wrong. Jinx missed the last two days of school, blaming it on being a woman. I'm not an idiot, and I hauled her ass into music with me. I know she's scared. Who wouldn't be? Some weird stalker has found her every single time, and we can't figure it out.

I'm watching her glare at Lula and this Piper chick. Honestly, they both give off some weird cult-like vibe. Why would they be chasing Von, of all professors? The guy is old and wrinkly. I'm sure his dick can't be that great. The thought of these two girls ruining any chance that Jinx had of getting out of this town breaks my heart, then again. I also signed up for the same thing—I'm no better.

"Baby, you need to ignore those two."

"That would be ideal if only I could. How can I compete when they go to dick town every chance they get. I still don't get how Piper is still here, and I told Dad about her days ago." She grips her bow tighter.

I pluck it from her hand. "We are partners, and we can beat Lula together. Shooting them the death glare hasn't worked, so let us try something else, yeah?"

I watch her breathe in, releasing a growl. "Fine." Her green eyes turn to me. "Get your stupid guitar out and play for me."

Okay, maybe the whole woman thing isn't a complete lie. She's acting all feral. Without arguing with her, I grab my guitar, giving it a quick tune. I know exactly what song to start playing. It's the song that started everything for me.

Heart-Shaped Box by Nirvana. I barely get a few chords played, and she smiles. She probably has no idea how much this song means to me; it pulled me out of some dark times.

"I'll repeat it, Maddox. You play that guitar like you were born with it."

"No, baby. You play like you were born with a cello. Now show those bitches where you belong." I give her a wink before falling back into the music.

We fill the room with our music, drowning out any conversation. The only one that matters is her and only her. I watch as her body sways with the music. I'll never tire of watching Jinx play, but playing with her will forever be my favorite. I've missed this more than I'll ever admit out loud.

The memories of that night of my attack try to break into my head; no matter what I do, I can't stifle those painful memories. Why did I have to be there that night? I could've practiced anywhere but the stupid music hall.

I did this to myself.

"Hey, are you all right?" Jinx's small hand lands on my thigh. "Did you want to get out of here?"

"Sorry, I got a bit distracted."

Her fingertips traced the edges of my scar. "Maddox." She slowly brushes each finger across my lower lip.

I snatch her wrist, halting her movement. Taking her finger into my mouth and biting the tip, I watch her green eyes dilate. "We should get out of here."

"Yeah, okay."

She goes about packing her cello away, and it still amazes me she can pack that massive case around for such a tiny thing. I'll always appreciate her musical talents and do what I can to see her succeed. But I still want that spot in the orchestra.

Does that make me a horrible person? I only want something good to happen in my life.

"What's the plan?"

"Heading back to your place. You're not allowed to be seen in public, remember?"

Her chest rises and falls. "Yeah, how can I forget? My life is now a living nightmare. I thought having Atticus here was a nightmare, but I was wrong."

I feel for her. I genuinely do. Unlike her, I left some of my nightmares at the old school. Those kids didn't follow me. After what Ace and Ash did to them, I'm surprised they even returned to school.

"When did you want to practice again? The orchestra will be here soon."

"My place is the safest, and no one goes up on my floor for a reason. No one likes the sound of a cello." She swings her case over her shoulder.

Lula and Piper giggle, and Jinx groans.

"Let's head out before I say something to the two bitch-es." She sends them a side-eye.

"I wouldn't stop you if you did." I take her cello case, drawing her into my arms. "But to be safe, we should leave."

She stares at the doors, and with a slight tug, she falls closer to my side, right where she belongs, where she should've been this entire time. The sun blinds us momentarily as we step outside—her body tenses.

"I won't let anything happen to you."

"I know, it's just." She looks around. "We don't even know who it is. How can you protect me?"

I grip her neck, tipping her jaw with my thumb. Her forest eyes clash with mine. "If I say I'll protect you, baby. I mean it. Some prick that hides behind a phone screen isn't going to scare me, and he shouldn't scare you."

She swallows hard, and the movement moves my hand. "Maddox, I can't ask you that. It's too much of a risk."

There isn't a way to explain it to her. The guys and I aren't risking anything for her; there isn't anything we wouldn't do for her. I only wish she would figure that out.

Reaching the dorms, I glance over my shoulder to make sure no one has followed us. I want to laugh since I have no idea who the fuck I'm looking for. As far as I know, the creep hasn't tried to contact her since wanting to meet her. I haven't asked either.

The best thing about her place is that there are no neighbors—the entire floor to herself, like a princess locked away in her tower. But Jinx isn't like a princess. She can rescue herself.

"How's Edgar?" I ask, opening her door.

"He's getting better. I'm sure he wants to get outside, but I'm worried he's not ready."

Edgar kraa's from his makeshift bed, poking his head up to check out who disturbed his slumber. Once satisfied, he dips down again. He's such a silly bird. When I look at Jinx, her lips draw a thin line.

"You Okay?"

Looking up at me, she nods. "Yeah, maybe a little tired. I'll get us something to eat. Are the twins joining us?"

"They should be here shortly."

Her shoulders drop. "I was hoping for a night with just you."

That'll never happen now. Those two will never leave her side, and I'm not only crazy about Odette but also obsessed. I have been since the first time I saw her in the backyard of her dad's place. Wearing black overall shorts with an off-the-shoulder black tee and all that beautiful dark hair tossed into a messy bun, I'll never forget how Jinx called me an asshole for trespassing without knowing who I was.

I watch as she mills around her little kitchen if you can call it a kitchen. It's like a small cutout in the room's corner with an L-shaped counter and a few cupboards. When she opens a cabinet, I hold back a laugh, and every shelf is filled with junk food.

She grabs a bag of chips, glancing over her shoulder. "Did you want something?"

I shake my head, laughing. "I'm worried I might dip into your apocalypse food."

Jinx looks back at her cupboard, then at me. "Nah, I have more down below. Spencer usually only takes me into the city once a month, so I make sure to grab a lot. But if the world were ending, we wouldn't starve."

"I believe it, but we would need more than sugar to survive."

She shrugs and heads to Edgar. She gives him a gentle pet before grabbing his treat off the small table under the window. He calls out, being impatient.

"You hush it, mister. I can only go so fast." She bends down, dropping the treat on his bed. Edgar dives fast, gobbling it up.

"All right, I need to ask. How did you befriend the bird?"

She watches Edgar, a small smile tugging at the corner of her mouth. "Do you believe in fate?" She rubs Edgar's head.

"I never gave it any thought. No." I move to the couch, waiting for her to tell her story.

A sigh escapes the confines of her mouth, and I watch as she lays next to Edgar's box. She unsnaps her fanny pack from around her waist and crosses her feet.

"When I first came here, Dad acted like I was an average person. He dropped me off at the front doors and drove away. He left me alone for the wolves." She waves her hand. "Anyway. This little rascal became a quick friend during my second week here, and he was only a chick. I think he tried leaving the nest too soon and couldn't fully fly yet. That's when I took him in. And you know what? I've been trying ever since to shake him, but he won't leave me alone." She laughs, giving Edgar a rub under his beak.

"And his name?"

She turns her head, raising her brow. "Seriously? Edgar Allan Poe. I don't think I need to spell it out, Maddox."

My body shook with the silent laughter; as her brows lowered, she rolled over. The look on her face is priceless.

"You do know who Poe is, correct?" her voice turned serious.

I lick my lips and grin. "I'm not that stupid, baby." I lean forward, resting my elbows on my knees, my eyes focusing intently on her face. "Once upon a midnight dreary, while I pondered, weak and weary, over many a quaint and curious volume of forgotten lore."

I watch her skin tighten with goosebumps. "Well, fuck me. Aren't we just full of surprises, Maddox Van Daren?"

She has no idea.

Three

Jinx

There are times in your life when you have to look back and wonder. If I had changed even a second, could things have gone differently? If I had woken up five minutes earlier, could that have been enough to change the entire day?

Perhaps if I hadn't come to this school, my life wouldn't be crumbling. It's all too late now. Whatever happens, I'm fucked. *Unknown* hasn't contacted me for three days, and I feel like I'm losing my mind. Every time my phone goes off, my stomach sinks, wondering if this is the time he finally has enough and is going to come and attack me.

I've never felt so surrounded yet alone when the guys are around. I refused to leave my room for days after standing *Unknown* up. Too afraid of what he would try, the guys tried everything they could think of to get me to leave, but I wouldn't change it. Even Spence tried bribing me with a trip into the city.

Nothing worked.

Then Maddox reminded me of Lula and Piper, and that was all the fire I needed to get my ass back to class.

The only issue I have now is when I do want to be alone, they won't let me. Atticus was pissed with me for hiding away from him, and he refuses to eat at his dorm for dinner now.

Atticus walks into my dorm, his ice-blue eyes clash with mine, and that cocky smirk pulls across his lips. Cause he knows he won again.

I sit up, crossing my legs, watching the twins place bags on the coffee table.

Ashton hauls out the takeout containers from the food court. The room is filled with the delicious smell of Chinese food. My stomach rumbles, reminding me it's been hours since I've last eaten anything.

"Here, grim."

He holds out a plate of food for me. "Thanks." I reach for it, but he doesn't let go.

"Are you doing okay?"

With a tight-lipped smile, I nod. "I'm trying, Ash. I have so many questions, no place to start, and the fact that it's been pure silence from him. That's what is eating at me."

He places the plate on the table and sits beside me. He runs his hand through my hair, pulling me closer to his side. My body relaxes into his side.

"We'll find him. We won't let anything happen to you, Jinx. You know that, right?"

I shrug. My brain agrees, but my heart doesn't. Something deep down is nagging at me; why hasn't he contacted me yet?

"Eat, Jinx. Then we can talk." Atticus slides my plate to the edge of the table. "I can't talk on an empty stomach."

I grab the plate, rolling my eyes. I've seen Atticus talk for hours without eating a bite; I know what he's trying to do. He's lucky that I'm letting him get his way. Without another word, I dig into my fried rice. I'm only eating to make him happy. When I look up from my plate, the guys are staring.

"What now?" I wave my fork in the air, getting annoyed.

Maddox smirks and Ashton shrugs. But fuckin' Atticus stares back. He sure knows how to get under my skin. I forcefully shove another forkful of rice into my mouth, never taking my eyes off Atticus. I can't help it. I give him the biggest smile in return. If he can't tell me what he wants, that's not my problem.

My phone dings from inside my fanny pack, and nobody moves for what feels like an eternity. My bag sits next to me, tormenting me. Did *Unknown* finally get tired of waiting around? Placing my plate on the floor, I reach for my phone. My fingers shake as I try to unzip my stupid fanny pack.

"Hold up, Jinx." Atticus stops me before I can retrieve my phone.

"Why?" I look up at him—his brow furrows when he tries to answer. Ashton moves for my pack, grabbing my phone. I hold my breath, waiting for disaster to strike.

Then Ashton laughs.

"How well do you know your friend, Spencer?" he asks.

"Pretty good. Why?" I try to reach the phone, but he holds it over his head.

"He sent you a selfie, and I'm unsure how to feel about it."

Oh, dear God. It could be anything from Spence. I wouldn't put it past him to send a dick pic just to get a reaction out of me and for me to storm down and talk to him. I grab the phone and stare at the screen.

I'm greeted with a picture of Spence sitting on the toilet with his pants down. He holds an empty toilet roll, pouting and giving me puppy dog eyes.

Pencil: I'm out. Got any up in the tower?

Me: Are you kidding? A selfie! You could've just asked for TP!

Pencil: Yeah, but this way, you can see my face. Haven't you missed me?

I look back at Ashton, and he quirks a brow. "I need to go visit Spence. Are you guys fine here?"

"Seriously? We were in the middle of supper?" Atticus snaps.

I grip my fork tight. "And I'm going to see my friend. You can't expect me to always hang out with you three. I did have a life before you all started here."

Maddox stands, heading to where I'm standing, and reaches for me. "I'll walk her down. Calm yourself, Ace. She won't be alone."

Atticus rolls his eyes and goes back to eating. Whatever, I don't have time for his mini meltdown. Atticus should remember this next time he runs out of toilet paper and texts me. Maybe I'll be too busy to deliver. Taking Maddox's hand, he lifts me off the floor with ease. I make my way to the bathroom and grab Spence a couple of rolls. Dickhead should go shopping if he ran out this fast.

Maddox doesn't speak until we're in the stairwell.

"Does Spencer usually send you bathroom selfies?"

I can't help but laugh. "Regarding Spence, you can't let your guard down. He's unpredictable. In a good way, don't get me wrong. Do you know what I mean? You have the twins and would do anything for them, even if it's stupid. Like, deliver toilet paper."

Maddox rubs my back, chuckling. "Yeah, you're right. But I don't think I would send a selfie."

"Can you send me a selfie?" I grin when he snaps his head toward me.

"Ah, what kind of selfie, Jinx?" His hand moves lower down my back, settling just above my ass.

I shrug. "You know, any selfie. But a sexy one would be nice." I push the door for the fourth floor open, moving away from his hold. I hear Maddox groan as I keep walking away from him toward Spence's dorm room.

"You can't walk away from me after that," he calls out.

I punch in the code into Spence's keypad. "Sure I can. Surprise me one day, and maybe I'll send one back."

I hear him swear under his breath, but I'm too busy staring at the mess of Spencer's place. He usually keeps this place clean, but holy shit. His clothes are thrown across the couch; dirty dishes lie around the coffee table and his desk. A mountain of garbage lays underneath it, and to be honest, I'm not sure what sticky shit I just stepped in.

"Spencer Aaron Coldwell!" I yell. As much as I'm going to regret this, I move toward the bathroom.

"Odette Morella Hawthorne, what took you so long? My ass and legs are numb."

I crack the bathroom door and throw his stupid toilet paper inside.

"Thanks, sugar tits. I'll be out soon."

"Wash your hands after." Guys are gross. I found Maddox, where I left him by the door. He's still taking in the room's sight. He hasn't turned away from the mess. I walk closer, placing my hand on his back, causing him to jump.

"Hey, are you okay?" I whisper.

"I'm fine," he replied slowly, his eyes evading mine.

I wrap my arm around his waist, pulling him into a hug. "If you ever need to talk, remember I'm here."

He digs his fingers into my hair, gripping a handful. He tilts my head back, and he stares into my eyes. With a deep sigh, he drops his forehead to mine. "I don't deserve you in my life, Jinx."

"Whenever you two lovebirds are finished, we can talk," Spence interrupts.

Maddox gives me a slight smirk before backing away. I take that chance to glare at Spence.

Spence throws his hands up in surrender. "Woah, Teeny. I had to interrupt before you two decided to fornicate on my couch."

If he only knew that Maddox and I haven't done that yet. The only one I have slept with so far is Atticus. Don't get me wrong, I'm not in this entire relationship to have sex, but I wouldn't mind exploring more with Maddox and Ashton.

"No offense, Spencer. But I wouldn't be touching that couch, man," Maddox tells him. Looking at the couch in disgust.

"I've been busy and haven't had time to clean. Don't judge me." He looks away, cringing.

I look around more, taking it all in. "Busy doing what—or who?"

Spence exhales loudly. "Not who, unfortunately. Just playing games and streaming late."

"Jesus Christ, Spence."

"I can leave you here and head back upstairs if you want more time to hang out?" Maddox turns his head my way.

I bit my lip. I turn back to Spence, and he's grinning like a kid on Christmas morning. I roll my eyes and laugh. "I'll stay. I need some time alone with my bestie. Thanks, Maddox."

His mouth hovered inches away from mine. "Stay inside until one of us comes for you, got it?"

"Yeah." I breathe out.

He dropped a quick kiss before walking away. Spencer lets out a low whistle.

I snap my finger at him. "Shut that pie hole and clean this fucking mess."

How did I end up with a bunch of men in my life again?

Four

Ashton

The door barely closes, and Atticus is already up and storming around Jinx's small living room. The poor bird keeps watching him every time he passes his box, and I swear he'll end up getting whiplash. I'm getting amusement out of this entire situation. Atticus needs to learn to let go of control. He isn't always in control, especially when it comes to her.

That's the one thing about my brother that drives me up the wall. The need for control, and I know the thought of a stalker out there still kills him. I told him already that finding the prick would take time. Then again, Ace listens to no one.

"How long does it take to drop ass wipe off?" he snaps at me.

"Hey, fuck you. I thought you were trying to be a nice guy. What happened to that?"

He waves me off. "That's only when Jinx is around. Besides, you already know I'm an asshole. Why sugarcoat it?"

I relax on the couch, resting my head on the back cushion. My eyes slowly droop close. I shouldn't be this tired; the stupid swim practices are kicking my ass. It doesn't help that my head hurts somewhat from being smashed into the side of the pool.

Ace digs his fingers into my shoulder. "Head hurting?"

"A little. I'll be fine."

"We'll figure out who did this, and we still need to deal with Liam. I'm not done tormenting Cameron, either. I won't be until he's groveling at my feet." His voice had a savage edge.

I keep my eyes closed, bringing my hand up to his and squeezing it. "Thanks, brother."

I'm jolted awake when the door slams closed. I blink a few times, trying to find my bearings, when I realize I'm still in

Jinx's place. Maddox now takes the position of pacing the room. Rubbing my face, I try to wake up; that's one thing I hate about naps is they mess with your inner clock.

"Maddox, what's going on?" I mumble. Watching him closely; even Ace does, too. My eyes follow Maddox across the room, waiting for him to answer.

Maddox lets out a frustrated groan, running his hands through his hair. "Spencer's place gave me flashbacks to my parent's house. It was a mess, and I know he isn't always like that, but my mind couldn't look past that. I had to leave before I mentally broke down in front of Jinx and Spencer."

"Do you need anything?" Atticus asks cautiously.

I dig into my pocket, pulling out a joint. "You can smoke it in the laundry room. Go relax for a minute before Jinx comes back. I take it that's why you came back alone?"

He walks closer to me, plucking the joint from my hands. "I had to. It was that, or do something stupid."

"How about you two go smoke, and I'll wait for Jinx downstairs. I don't want her walking back alone, anyway." Atticus suggests.

I shrug, getting up. I'm always up for smoking; besides, it may help Maddox with whatever is going through his head. I've been in the depths of the mind, and it's hard to get out. Once that dark hole grabs you, it can take all your willpower to fight for your life. Even now, it's a fight not to return.

We don't talk until we reach the laundry room. Thankfully, it's empty. Lighting up the joint, I quickly take a puff before passing it to Maddox.

"Wanna talk about it?"

He exhales a cloud of smoke, and his shoulders sink. "Ash, the demons are banging at the door, and I'm not sure I can hold them back anymore. Jinx found my room a disaster after I went on a bender. She never said I disappointed her, but how could you not be? Then, to have her find me in the bathroom. I can't be the guy she needs right now."

"So, what's your plan? Ditch out?"

He walks around the small laundry room, taking another puff, swinging to look at me, smoke curling from his lips. "What do you want from me?"

I storm closer to him, snatching the joint from his fingers. "I want you to man up and own your shit. Talk to Jinx. You know she won't judge you. She's not like that." I watched as he struggled to keep the tears at bay. "Maddox, she won't leave you," I spoke gently this time.

"What if she does? She did before."

I pull him close, crushing my arms around him. His body shakes as mine breaks for him. No matter how often I tell him he's good enough or no one will leave him, he'll never believe me. The demons refuse to leave him alone. I'm afraid that one day they'll win. I was lucky. Atticus saved me when I hit rock bottom after that night.

"Come on, let's get you back upstairs. I think you should stay with Jinx tonight," I say, steering him toward the door.

"No, I can't."

I tug him harder. "Don't care, and neither will Jinx. Sleep on the fucking couch for all I care."

Maddox slowly trudges out of the laundry room; I catch a glimpse of a body rounding the corner down the hall, probably someone wanting to do laundry.

We walk shoulder to shoulder up the stairs. My mind keeps trying to return to that night; Maddox isn't the only one who drinks the demons away when no one is looking. Passing Spencer's place, I notice Atticus isn't there. That can only mean that he and Jinx are back in her room. I can only hope he isn't being a dick about her hanging out with Spencer.

"Sorry about everything back there. I didn't mean to cry."

"Mad, that's what friends are for. Anytime you need the shoulder, it's there."

He simply nods, then opens Jinx's door, and we freeze. I walk in slowly, never taking my eyes off Ace or Jinx.

"What happened?" I collapse next to Jinx, taking her hand. "Little swam. Talk to me." I gently caress her cheek, wiping away a tear.

Maddox leans over the armrest, brushing away her air. "Baby, please."

I send a glare to Ace. He's the one that was with her. "What the fuck did you do to her?"

"Hey! I didn't do shit this time," he snaps. "I was waiting outside Spencer's room when she opened the door paler than Casper. She hasn't spoken a word." His eyes never leave Jinx as he finishes talking.

"You don't think Spence tried anything, do you?" Maddox lowers his voice.

Atticus growls. "If he did, he's dead."

I shake my head. "No. Trust me. I know the signs of sexual assault. This is something else." My mind flashes with all the possibilities that it could be. What could've happened in his room? We weren't gone very long for shit to hit the fan. All they were doing was cleaning.

"Where's her phone?" I watch her eyes grow wide. "Jinx, what are you hiding? You need to talk to us. You need to talk. We can't help you otherwise."

Tears drop onto the cushion, but she doesn't speak.

"Here, I have it," Maddox calls out behind me.

I turn around, and Jinx squeezes my hand hard. I soothe the back of her hand with my thumb. I wait for Maddox to read whatever awaits us.

"Jesus fucking Christ." He drew in his breath sharply. "He sent this today?—of course, he did."

"Read it," Ace demands, losing his patience with Mad.

Maddox sits on the coffee table, leaning on his thighs. With a deep breath, he reads. "Odette, I'm disappointed in you. We made a date, and you stood me up. I don't like to be made a fool. The next time that happens, punishment will occur."

Three days. She lasted three days from that prick.

"What did I do? Did I dress a certain way? Or did I tell a guy no? I don't understand."

I climb over Jinx, tugging her back to my chest. Maddox holds her hand, and Atticus stays where he is. His body vibrated with anger.

"Listen to me, Jinx. You did nothing wrong. Some people develop an obsession that can't be explained, that's all. You can have my phone." I try to reassure her, but even I can't be sure that'll work.

"We stick to what we've been doing, and you don't leave our side. If we can't be with you." Ace rubs his forehead. "Call us and stay on the phone until you reach your room or class. Never be alone."

Maddox leans closer to Jinx, his eyes raking hers. "I'm staying here tonight. Is that alright with you?"

She reaches out and strokes his cheek. "I don't mind at all."

That's my sign to leave. I slowly turned her head. A tiny worm of doubt gnawed at me. Sooner or later, she'll want to take this relationship to the next step, and I'll have to tell her my darkest secret. Will she still want me after? The thought alone makes my stomach turn. I quickly press my lips to hers and move away from her.

I don't bother to look at my brother as I walk out of the room. I need some air; being in that room is beginning to suffocate me. I need to clear my head.

The only spot I can think of heading to is the pool. Being in the water is calming, and I can't wait until tomorrow for practice. The pool is empty when I walk into the center. The chlorine fills my nose, bringing back familiar memories—some good and some I want to bury. Especially with Cam and Liam, those assholes need to pay.

I step into the locker room; the peacefulness of being here is welcoming. Opening my locker, I find my black Speedo waiting for me. Grovedale loved their blue briefs, but the black will forever be my favorite. Stepping to the pool's edge, I watch the water stand still.

Slicing through the water, it soothes me. With each stroke, my mind calms down. I'm not sure how many laps I end up doing, but when I grip the edge of the pool, Atticus is there.

"Ash. Where's your head at?" He never takes his eyes off me. He was probably wondering if I was about to drown myself.

"Between my shoulders, don't worry. I'm fine." I pull myself out of the pool, grabbing the towel off the benches. "Trust me, Ace. I'm not going to off myself."

"It's almost been two years." His voice was nothing but a whisper.

I wrap the towel around my waist, facing him. "Yes, thank you. I'm aware of the night some bitch raped me."

I storm off toward the locker room, and he doesn't need to remind me constantly. I know I'm the damaged twin; I let some college girl spike my drink and take advantage of me. Thanks. I got the memo two years ago when I woke up with my pants around my ankles and couldn't remember anything. It wasn't hard to figure it out when the chick was still lying beside me.

Pushing those memories deep again, I get dressed. I don't want to think that was the point of coming here tonight.

Fuck Atticus and his big mouth.

Five

Jinx

Last night was a whirlwind. I let my emotions get in the way. I never should have let *Unknown* get a reaction out of me. He doesn't deserve that. The only response he deserves is anger. I'll rain down on him next time. Fuck him.

I quietly get out of bed, trying not to wake Maddox, and make my way to the small kitchen. Edgar doesn't waste any time hopping over and squawking.

"Yeah, I got it." I'm confident the little fucker is healed, but he's milking it. He's only staying behind because of all the treats he gets. I open his treat jar, and he hops on the table.

"Gwah."

"Don't you start, or I'll kick you out." I drop Edgar's treat on the table, and when I turn around, I bump into a hard, naked chest.

"You wouldn't kick my bud out over a treat, would you, baby?" Maddox tips my chin up. His lips curl with a smirk.

I pat his cheek. "Listen here. He's giving me a hard time."

"Don't be dramatic. Edgar is wounded." He lays his hand on the table, and Edgar steps inside his palm. What a little trader.

"You two can have your bro time. I'm getting dressed. I have an early class." I leave, letting them enjoy their time. One thing I hate about morning classes is they are too early. I enjoy sleeping in. Opening my dresser drawer, I pull out a pair of black lace underwear and a matching bra. Stripping off my sleep set, a deep groan comes from the doorway.

"God, Jinx. You could bring me to my knees, and I wouldn't complain."

Goosebumps work down my body as Maddox pushes off the doorframe. My nipples draw tight the closer he gets. The way Maddox looks at me reminds me that nothing else matters. It's only him and I, and nothing will come between that.

He reaches out, dragging his hand down my arm until his fingers tangle with mine, making me drop my bra and underwear on the floor. His hazel eyes burned into mine, and with a slit tug, my body pressed against his. I wrap my arms around his waist and the muscles in his back flex under my fingertips.

"Jinx, I need you, please."

I work my hands up his back, tilting my head back, and he stares at me. "You have me, Maddox. I'm all yours."

"Good, now open your legs for me. Let me feel that wet pussy again."

I slowly spread my legs, waiting for him. Fuck the early class. I don't need business management, anyway. Maddox drags his finger along my collarbone, never taking his eyes off mine. I need him to go faster, I won't be able to control myself.

I go to move my hand from his neck, and he stops. "Move your hands, and this is over."

All I can do is nod, curling my fingers into his hair. Threading them deeper, I wait patiently for him to move; each passing second feels like a lifetime.

"Maddox, move already."

His upper lip curls into a smirk. "No, maybe not." He pulls back, and my hands drop.

"Are you kidding me?" I cry in protest, throwing my hands in the air. "I've wanted you for years, Maddox, and now you're turning me away?"

His hand moves fast, gripping the back of my neck and swatting my pussy with his other hand. I cry out in pain, drawing in a shaky breath. His eyes hold mine as his finger slips deep inside.

"This pussy is mine." He pumps his finger fast, as my pussy tightens. My fingers cling to the waistband of his jeans. When he adds another finger, my legs tremble. Just when I was about to come, he pulls away.

"No," I cry out in outrage.

"You're coming on my dick or nothing, baby." He unzips his jeans, slipping them down past his hips. I watch like a greedy, hungry wolf. I wait, then I drop to my knees; taking hold of his dick, he lets out a low moan.

"God, I love your touch. Jinx." He groans when I stroke him slowly. He gathers my hair into a tight pony and pushes my face closer to his dick. I stick my tongue out, licking from the base to the tip, then swallow him deep in my mouth. His hold tightens the more I suck him off. If he thinks I'll let him finish, he's wrong. I push against his thighs, popping him from my mouth.

"You're not finishing in my mouth. I want your cum dripping from my pussy all day."

"Fuck, baby. You're damn right, I want my cum dripping from you. Every step you take." He pulls my hair, so I stand. "Every time you sit." His hands slide down my ass, lifting me. "I want you to remember who made you so wet."

I wrap my legs around his waist, working my hand between us. I line him up, and he drops me slowly, stretching me; I thought Atticus was big, but Maddox is thicker.

"Maddox." I moan his name.

He grips my ass tight, flexing his hips fast. "God. I've waited forever to feel your pussy on my dick. I was stupid to wait so long."

Tangling my fingers in his hair, I move my hips faster. "Shut up and fuck me. We can talk later."

"I can do that." He walks over to the bed, tossing me down. "Roll over. I'll show you fucking."

I lick my dry lips; this will be new to me. Not being able to see him is scary. What if he tries something? I'll never know. My chest tightens when I try to draw in a breath. Maddox's hand runs down my back, sending shivers racing down my spine.

"Get out of your head, Jinx. I'm not going to do anything to hurt you. I would never do that." His body pressed against mine; his weight pushes me further into the mattress—calmness eases over me.

"I'm good. I've only ever had sex twice. Atticus is a force to reckon with. I'm sorry, talking about another guy probably isn't good for your ego." I push my face into the blanket.

He laughs, pressing his face into my neck. "Baby, I know how Atticus is. You talking about him while we're both naked isn't going to scare my hard-on away. Did you want to try this position, or did you want to face me?"

"I'll try this one." The words barely leave my lips, and his hand slips between my legs. He drives two fingers into my wet, aching core. "Holy shit." I moan out, pressing more into him.

"Are you ready?" He moves away, pulling his fingers out.

"Yeah, if you are." I tip my head to get a look at him.

He smiles. "I'm always ready."

He buries himself deep inside, and my body explodes with ecstasy. His hands pull my ass into his hips, driving his dick deeper. The sound of his groans causes my core to clench.

"Touch yourself. I wanna feel that pussy choke my dick until I'm spilling deep inside you."

I don't think I need to touch myself to come; the way he talks is enough for me. I slip my hand between, finding my clit with my finger—I rub. My back arches, and Maddox hisses as I climb closer to the finish line. He thrusts faster and lifts my leg onto the bed, getting better access to my g-spot. I keep rubbing my clit, air catches in my lungs, and I scream into the mattress. Maddox rocks slowly, his fingers digging into my skin. With a final slam, he groans, spilling into me.

I try to even out my breathing when warm lips press against my back.

"I think you missed your morning class, baby." He pulls out, lying next to me. "Do you need your inhaler?"

"No. I'm fine. If I'm quick enough, I can catch my other morning class." I roll onto my back, covering my eyes. My chest is tight but manageable. I don't want to leave; reality will smack me in the face once I step outside. My small safe bubble will burst, as much as I don't want to. I need to talk to Dad.

"I'll walk you to class. Soon, this bullshit will be over."

Pipe dream. This won't end until my stalker creep finally has what he wants. I slip out of bed, heading back to the dresser. I bend down, picking up my discarded underwear. Without paying attention to Maddox and his groaning, I slip them on.

"You're killing me, baby. I should bend you over and fuck that sweet pussy again."

I ignore him, walking to the closet instead. I want to step out in public like a normal person and not be worried about being watched or having a text sent to me with a picture saying *he could be better*. Or worried if I kiss one of the guys, I might piss *Unknown* off. These things shouldn't be in the front of my mind. I pull on a short black skirt and an oversized sweater.

"Jinx, talk to me. What's going on?" Maddox meets me outside my closet, already dressed, holding my mini bookbag.

"Nothing is wrong." I swipe my bag from his hand. I go to move to the bathroom, but he blocks me.

"Start talking. We were doing great, and then the next thing I know, you shut down. If I did something wrong or hurt you, please tell me."

"It's not you." I snap. "Everything is happening so fast. I haven't had time to think or breathe. I feel like I'm losing my goddamn mind, Maddox."

"I'm sorry, Jinx. Truly, I am. I would snap my fingers and take care of this asshole, but Atticus is trying to figure it out. We need more time. Can you give us that?"

"I get that it's only been a few weeks, but it feels like months. It feels like he's been one step ahead of me. I hope Ash can change my number, which can give me some peace for a little while." Maddox pulls me into his chest, and my arms naturally find his waist. He gently kisses my forehead, guiding me to the bathroom.

"I'll be in the living room. Take some time."

I wait until he's gone and stare at myself in the mirror. Things were going great until the guys showed up, but maybe it was already in effect beforehand, and with them showing up, my stalker felt threatened; that's why he's taking action.

I'm still convinced it's Cameron.

He's the only one who acted interested in me, the only one who's ever talked to me besides Spencer. Who else could it be? That asshole has it coming, that's for sure. The next time I see Cam, he has some questions to answer, too.

Six

Jinx

I tell Maddox I need to see Dad and not to wait around. I'm unsure how long this will take or if he can see me today. I'm not even inside the office, and Florence pops her head up, and her smile widens.

"Good morning, my dear. The dean is busy, but between you and me, the outcome should be amazing." I move toward her desk, wondering who he's talking to. I hope it's stupid, Von. Then again, that would never happen.

"Why?" I drag out.

"I heard a little incident happened during the swim practice, and the coach didn't do anything. So." She leans back, checking the hall to the dean's office. "He's replacing him with a retired Olympic coach. Isn't that amazing?"

My heart squeezes tight. I was honestly hoping Dad would replace Von. The sleaze ball needs to go; how hard is it to find a qualified music teacher? Don't get me wrong, I'm glad that Ash will hopefully figure out which douche-canoe tried to take him out, but I need this more.

"Florence, that is great. The coach is horrible and picks favorites. I'm glad that the swim team will be getting a clean-up, especially a qualified coach."

She pats my hand. "I'm sure a certain music teacher will be next, Hun. It just takes time to find the right fit."

"I know, it just sucks. I've been here longer, and it seems like my stepbrothers are getting everything."

"It may seem like that, but it's not. Have patience."

"I'm tired of that word. Patience takes forever sometimes." I return to the seats, feeling deflated that I might miss out again on the orchestra.

Florence goes back to typing, ignoring me. We've grown accustomed to each other; we don't need to fill every second with conversation. I text the boys quickly, telling them I'll be in the office for a while and not to worry about meeting me at my class.

I browse the *Darwin School of Music,* checking out their classes, dreaming of the day I'll finally walk the halls. RWA can only prepare me so much with my music; I need to further it, and only three people stand in my way. Lula, Piper, and Von.

I need to take out Lula and Piper first, and if Von won't leave, then I'll simply make him. Prescott Hawthorne isn't the only one with the power at this school. If only I weren't scared to use that power, I promised Dad that no one would find out.

Voices pull me from my phone. When I look up, Cam and Liam walk into the office.

"Well, if it isn't Jinx, the minx. It's been a while, doll." His chocolate brown hair must always be perfectly styled, not a strand out of place. I guess when your family has ties to the school, your presentation is important.

"Not long enough." I roll my eyes, going back to my phone. Of course, that's not enough for him to steer clear of me. He could never learn the word. No.

He plucks my phone from my hand. I reach for it, but he tucks it in his back pocket.

"Give it back, you asshole."

He waves his finger at me. "Not until you agree to go out on one date." He smirks.

"Never gonna happen, Cam. Give me back my phone." I hold my hand out, waiting. When he doesn't move, I snap my fingers, getting impatient. "Give it. The date will never happen."

Florence clears her throat. "Cameron and Liam, what can I do for you, gentlemen?"

Cameron loses focus, and I snatch my phone back. His hand reaches out, grabbing my wrist. His nails dig into my skin. I try to pull back, but it only makes him grip me tighter.

"Don't even think about it," he murmurs, his head slightly bowed

"Ms. Florence." Liam interrupts. "We need a new schedule for the swim team. Coach hasn't updated ours."

Florence presses her glasses up, lowering her head back to her keyboard. "Have a seat, gentlemen. The dean will see you soon."

Cameron lets go of me finally, raising his hands. "What does that mean?" He bit off each word.

"It means wait your turn or leave," Florence tells him, not missing a beat.

I turn my body away from Cam, rubbing my wrist. Since the party, I made it a point to stay far away from him. Ever since the bathroom incident, I haven't been in the same room as him. I go to stand, and Cam slams his hand on my thigh, stopping me. My body tenses when his finger moves under my skirt.

"Where are you going?" he demands, with a feral look in his eyes.

Liam steps in front, blocking Florence's view. I cling to the armrest, staring at Liam's back, not moving as Cam slides his hand further up my thigh.

"See, I knew you wanted this, Jinx. Why fight me all this time?" He moves my hair away from my neck, rubbing his finger along my throat.

My stomach bottoms out; dread creeps in as I try to catch my breath. I feel nothing as he continues to stroke my neck. He moves closer, brushing his nose against my ear. I close my eyes, wishing my body would cooperate and move. I grip the chair tighter when I feel my body shake.

"Fuck, Jinx, you smell amazing," Cam whispers into my ear.

A sudden pain grips me by the throat when I try to tell Cam no. I'm screaming at my body to move away, to do something, but I'm rooted to my chair. Liam's body begins to blur, as tears roll down my cheek the more Cam strokes my neck.

His finger moves to my cheek, wiping away my tears. "Aw. What's wrong? I like you like this, not talking back."

His other hand hasn't moved any closer, but one slip and his finger could slip under my underwear. Fear turns my stomach, thinking about what he could do; no one would notice. A small whimper passes my lips, and Cam smirks. Finally, getting a reaction from me. His eyes glimmered with amusement.

Deep laughs come from the hall, distracting Cameron. I can finally fight my body and shove his hand from under my skirt. Drawing in a harsh breath, I turn to him.

"Touch me again, and you'll be sorry."

He flashed his teeth with a grin. "Don't make promises, Jinx."

Dad rounds the corner with the new coach, patting him on the shoulder like they are best friends. Liam and Cameron move quickly, cutting them off. My mind is racing with what just happened. I can't see Dad like this. He'll know something happened.

With shaky knees, I stand, trying to be quiet so they don't see me. I just rounded the chair.

"Odette. Did you need something?"

The sound of his voice makes me want to shatter. Staring at the door, I don't dare turn my head to look at him. The moment I do, I'll cry.

"No, Dean Hawthorne. I'll come back later." My lips trembled around the words.

"I'm sure she's fine, aren't you, Jinx." Cameron laughed as he spoke.

Taking careful steps, I make my way out of the office. I rush down the hall to the restroom, pushing the door open. My body slumps against the sink; with each breath, it feels like a boulder is on my chest. My fingers shake when I try to drag my bag off my shoulder. I can't believe I let that happen. I should've pushed Cameron away, but I sat there and let his greasy hands touch me. With numb fingers, I unzip the stupid bag and find my inhaler.

I stare at myself in the mirror as I take a puff of the inhaler. God, I'm so stupid. I should've left sooner or called for Florence. Things could've escalated more if Dad hadn't come down the hall when he did.

My phone buzzes, and my stomach sinks. I can't tell the guys what happened. I can't add another thing to our pile of stress. I don't even want to think about what occurred today. If I tell anyone, it would be Spence; he might give me some advice.

Atticus: Did you need me to walk you to your class?

All I want to do is go back to my room and hide.

Me: Sure, I'm by the office

Atticus: OK, I'll be there shortly. Don't move or talk to anyone.

I don't want to leave the restroom if Cam is still out there lurking. Atticus will know something happened. Cameron can't hold his tongue and needs to brag about everything. If I don't tell the guys, Cam will. I'm stuck in a hard place, and I'm not sure what to do.

My phone buzzes again.

"Jesus, Ace, I get it." I grab my phone again, and my world tilts.

Unknown: What a fuckin' show today in the office. I didn't think you would add another man to your group. Where can I sign up?

Me: Leave me alone.

Unknown: No Jinx. I think this photo I took will be my favorite from now on.

My stomach churns at the thought of him staring at a photo of Cam with his hand under my skirt. And I rush into the stall; my knees buckle, and I fall to the floor. Sweat runs down my back as I cling to the toilet bowl, and bile slicks the back of my throat, spilling into the water. I grab some toilet paper and wipe my chin. Leaning against the stall, I can't think about going out there now.

Atticus will for sure know something is up.

Seven

Atticus

I know I told Ash that I wasn't going to be an asshole, but my last nerve is beginning to waste away. When you tell me you're going to be some place, fuckin' be there. I try to take a calming breath but fuck that shit. I storm into the office to find Prescott, Cam, Liam, and some preppy douche who looks like he's trying too hard to get his youth back.

I feel like I stumbled into a secret society because no one has said anything. But the way Prescott is glaring at Cam, I can only imagine what the dipshit did this time. I still don't trust the prick or his little sidekick for what happened with Ash. One of them is guilty of drowning him, and I won't be holding back when I figure it out.

"Atticus, so good of you to join us." Prescott steps forward. "I was going to make introductions later, but since you're here. This is Bran. He'll be taking over as the new coach. Bran, this is Atticus Banks. He's one of our finest swimmers."

Bran reaches his hand out for mine, and even if I don't want to, I shake it.

"Finest? Is that so?"

"No. My brother is the best. If you can keep the team's captain from trying to kill him, that is." I quirk a brow at Cam. I want him to say something. Tell me that you did it. I'm waiting.

The coach turns his head to Cam, his eyes bore through him. "He did what now?"

"Don't listen to him. He's full of lies. It wasn't proven." Cam shoves me, moving me back. And my anger got the best of me. I moved to push him back when Prescott grabbed my shoulder.

"Woah. That's enough. Back away from each other."

I back away toward the door. "You watch your back, Cameron. Either he deals with you, or I will." I point to the new coach, looking him dead in the eyes. "Figure your shit out, or I'm off the team."

Cam can think that he won by hiding behind the coach, but I'll win. One way or another, he won't be smiling for long. When I step back into the hall, Jinx isn't there still. My blood boils even more. Where the fuck could she have gone? Pulling my phone out of my back pocket, I find her number. I'm tired of her shit, I get that she doesn't like us following her around, but that doesn't give her the right to ditch out on us. She knows anything can happen to her.

Her phone rings before going to voicemail. I hang up and call again. I head down the hall when I hear ringing from the girls' restroom. If she's hiding away from me, I swear to God. I crack my neck and breathe deeply. Pushing the door open, I step inside to find it empty.

I push each stall door open until I come to a locked one. "Jinx, I know you're in here. Come out before I drag you out." I shake the door, but she hasn't made a peep. "Jinx, fuckin' answer me." Sweat trickles down my spine, and my mind spirals back to when I found Ashton lying on the bathroom floor. I thought for sure that was the day I was going to lose my brother—if I was a minute late. My stomach sinks even further. Without thinking, I open the stall door, finding Jinx curled up on the floor.

I drop to my knees, gathering her up. "Little grim, tell me what happened?" My eyes roam over her face, trying to see if she's hurt. "Talk to me, please."

A grim expression cuts across her pale face. "I ran into Cam and Liam in the office."

I take a deep breath and control myself from going back in there. "What happened? And don't you dare lie to me."

She buried her face against my throat and groaned. "Cam was just being Cam."

"And I'm the Queen of England."

"She's dead!"

"Yeah, and so is Cam when I'm finished with him. Now tell me what he did." I weave my fingers in her hair, tugging her head back. Her eyes slowly close. "Jinx, don't make me work for the answer."

"I tried to stop him, but he wouldn't listen." Her eyes misted with tears.

I clench my teeth hard, trying not to lose control. But the longer she takes to explain right away, the more my mind wanders, my body locks in rage. "Touched you where Odette? Because I'm thinking the worst here."

She turns, reaching for her phone. I watch as she opens the screen to a text message with a picture of her sitting in the office with Cameron next to her. I rip the phone from her hands, getting a closer look, and I find that prick's hand under her skirt.

"Who sent the picture?" I squeeze her phone tight as I continue to stare at the photo.

"My stalker did."

My eyes snapped away from the phone to her. "You mean *Unknown* was this close to you? Jesus Christ, Jinx. And no one in the office noticed what was going on?"

She shakes her head. "Liam was blocking everything from Florence."

I open her group chat she has with us guys because I won't be able to stop myself if I go after Cameron alone.

Jinx: It's Ace. Meet me by the office ASAP.

I move to stand, but Jinx stops me. "What are you going to do?"

"Kill Cameron."

Maddox: On my way. What's going on?

"You can't kill him."

"Watch me."

Ashton: Same. Fill me in, bro.

"Backup is coming. Let's move it." I push off the floor, setting her on her feet. "Don't fight me on this. That asshole needs to pay for what he did."

She pulls my shirt, getting close to my face. "I said no killing, you'll ruin your future, and I'm not worth that."

"That's not up to you, and if you ever speak about yourself like that again. I'll spank you until your ass is red, and it hurts to sit. Now get in that hall and wait for the guys to arrive."

The only thing she needs to worry about is getting her ass back to her dorm. Cameron will be lucky to be sucking soup from his jaw once I'm finished with him. No one touches my girl, and can talk about it. Stepping out of the restroom, the guys are already waiting for us by the office. Maddox spots us first and snaps his eyes to Jinx.

"What the fuck happened?" he calls out as he storms close to us. He tilts her chin up, looking at her face. "Baby, talk to me."

Ashton hasn't moved from his spot. From the look on his face, he knows something horrible went down. Once he finds out precisely what happened, I don't think I'll be able to hold him back; he'll do more damage than I will.

She looks up at me, and I nod with understanding. "Maddox, take her to her room. I'll text you what happened."

"Yeah, okay." He wraps his arm around her shoulder. "I'll take care of her. You two do what needs to be done."

I watch them both walk away before moving to Ashton's side.

I watched as his nostrils flared. "Who?"

"Our favorite captain. He took it into his own hands to touch what's ours." I opened Jinx's phone and showed him the text. "Her stalker pal also had an eye full."

"Sonofabitch. Where is Cam now?"

"He was in the office, but if I would guess, he's at the house."

He scoffs, rolling his eyes. "He's such a pussy. I can't wait to put him in his place. I've been waiting since day one."

We take off for the Blackwood House. I'm glad we don't have to live there anymore. It's one of the things I'll love Prescott for. The other thing is for bringing Jinx into my life. I'll admit it's the only thing my mother did right.

With every step I take, the more my anger builds. It amazes me that Cam will still try and push the limit with us but to bring Jinx into this. I won't have it. She doesn't deserve that. The house comes into view, and Emery is sitting on the steps.

"Where's Cam?" Ash yells out.

"W-what?" Emery's head snaps up.

"Don't act stupid. You heard us. Where's the cunt hiding?" I storm past him, heading for the front door.

Emery stumbles up the stairs after us. "Wait, Atticus. Stop." He reaches for me, but I turn the handle, pushing the door open.

The house is dark, and a party hasn't been held in weeks, which is odd for Cam. From what we were told, he usually hosts one almost every week. He's gone downhill since before the swim meet, but that won't stop me from busting his face.

"Cameron! I know you're in here. Get your ass down here!" I holler up the stairs.

"If you were a smart man, you would find him for us," Ashton tells Emery.

Emery shakes his head. "You don't get it. The new coach let him go as captain. Cameron isn't taking it well."

"I guess that's too bad for him. Get him in here." I slowly turn my head to face Emery. "Or you'll take his beating."

He points to the patio door. "He's out back."

Ashton rushes for the door, slides it open, and doesn't stop. I ran to catch up to him.

"You fuckin touched my girl?" He rips Cams out of the lounger, getting into his face. "Didn't we tell you already not to go anywhere near her?"

Cam tries to shove Ash away, but Ash holds tight. "Get off me, you psycho. You don't own a person."

I stand behind Cam and nod at Ash to release him. Cam turns around, and his face pales. He goes to move, but I copy him. He isn't going anywhere.

"I can own her, and what we say goes." Cam doesn't have time to register that I'm swinging my arm. All the rage I've been holding in collides with his jaw. He falls to the ground, grabbing his face. Ashton jumps in, kicking him in the ribs.

"You fucked with the wrong Banks, prick." Ashton smashes his foot into Cam's side again. I hold Ash back, letting Cam breathe for a second.

"Fuck you," he wheezes out. He rolls onto his knees, coughing. "You aren't gonna keep me away from her."

"Think again." I grip his hair, expose his face, and slam my fist into his jaw again. The sound of his jaw breaking makes my heart happy. He grabs his face and cries in pain.

"I suggest you get someone to drive you to the hospital quickly." Ashton shoves him as he walks by.

Emery stares wide-eyed as we walk past him.

"You okay, brother?" Ash asks as we step out the front door.

I flex my hand. "I'm fine. I swear if Cameron touches or talks to her once more, he's fuckin' dead."

I shouldn't have to tell him. I only share amongst my circle. Even then, it's hard to imagine Maddox or Ashton touching Jinx. I remind myself that they won't steal her away from me, that they love her as I do and would do anything for her.

Eight

Maddox

Jinx never said a word the entire time as we walked back to the dorm. I tried to rein in my anger and not go after Cameron myself, but knowing Ash and Ace, they would take care of him. Cam would be stupid to try anything with her again. The thought of having her stalker friend inches away from her makes my stomach turn. He could've tried anything, and we wouldn't have known. She wouldn't have known it was him either.

I tried to talk to Jinx as we walked up the stairs, but she still wouldn't say anything. Even after getting her inside her room, nothing. I'm beginning to worry that she'll never talk to me again. I should've been there, but she said she was fine waiting in the office to speak to her dad and for me to attend class.

This is my fault. I slam my fist into her door, not giving a shit that it's a steel door.

"Odette, I'm so fuckin' sorry. I should've been there." I punch the door again, and my knuckles scream in pain. But it's nothing compared to what Jinx has gone through.

I slowly turn to face her, and she's standing in front of her sink, gripping the counter until her knuckles have turned white.

"This isn't your fault, Maddox." She grits her teeth. "I should've left the office, but my stupid body wouldn't let me. I sat there frozen while Cameron touched me. I'm to blame for this."

"Don't you fucking say that. If I can't blame myself, neither can you. Even though I should've stayed."

She tilts her head back and sniffs. "Why can't I catch a break, Maddox?" she asks, a sob catching in her throat.

I cross the room, drawing her into my chest. "Sometimes, the toughest soldiers are dealt the most brutal battles."

"I would like to be discharged from service, please." She squeezes me tighter.

"I'm sorry, baby. I promise it'll get easier." I pulled back, giving her a tender smile. "Let me start the shower for you and get you out of these clothes and into something more comfortable."

"Thanks, Mad." A small smile touches her mouth.

I walk her to the bathroom and turn the shower on. I leave her alone, as much as I hate it. I hope Ash and Ace make Cameron pay for what he did to her. Just thinking about it makes my stomach turn. I'm not sure why he's so fascinated with her.

I'm washing my bloody hand off when the door swings open, and the twins come storming in, arguing.

"Shut the fuck up, Ash. I handled it. We won't get into trouble."

"That's what you think. Do you know who he's related to? Prescott will be up our asses soon."

"Like I give a shit. Once he finds out what he did to Jinx, it's game over for Cameron."

My head swivels between them, trying to catch up with their conversation, but I'm lost.

"What's going on?"

"Atticus broke Cameron's jaw." Ashton swings his hands in the air.

I don't see a problem. "Okay and?" I give them a confused look.

Atticus rolls his eyes. "Cameron is a legacy."

"Which means we are up shit creek without a paddle," Ashton adds, glaring at his brother.

Atticus drops onto the couch, folding his ankle over his knee. "We aren't getting into trouble. Drop it, Ashton.

That prick had it coming. End of story. I can't keep arguing with you."

"I have to agree. Prescott isn't going to do shit once he finds out. Why are you so worried?" I carefully dry my hands off, watching Ashton have a mental breakdown.

"He's worried because the last time they did something stupid, Dad gave them an alternative. Plus, Cam's grandfather has some major strings at this school that even Dad can't pull."

We all turn to look at Jinx. She's standing in the small hallway, wearing a pair of black sweatpants and Atticus' hoodie, and her hair is wrapped up in a towel. My heart skips a beat when her green eyes meet mine.

"What do you mean? Doesn't your dad own this school?" Ace asks, raising a pale blond brow.

She scoffs, moving further into the room. "He does, but that doesn't mean shit when he bought it from the school board. He still has to answer to all the members; I'm not sure what will happen."

The door opens as if he were summoned. Prescott stands there with a blank stare and slowly turns, taking in Jinx. Closing his eyes, he rubs his forehead.

"Jesus Christ. I'm a shitty father."

Jinx rushes to him, wrapping her arms around him; he wraps his arms around her shoulders, dropping his face into the towel around her head.

"It's not your fault, Dad."

"I was in the office and didn't even notice you were." He pulls her closer, taking a deep breath. His eyes meet Atticus', then Ashton's.

"What do you know?" I asked, moving to the small chair.

"Tell me what I should know. I just got a call from Cameron's grandfather naming my sons as the attackers."

Atticus licks his lips and stands. "You should sit."

Prescott pushes Jinx arm's length away. "What did that asshole do to you? Because scenarios are running through my head that no father wants to be thinking, and I won't be able to control my next move if I get my hands on that SOB."

Jinx dips her head and threads her fingers together. "Dad, it's not where your mind is going, but it's not that far off."

Prescott blows a puff of air out. "How far off?"

Jinx turns to us, chewing her lip.

"He touched her in your fuckin office," Ashton spits out.

Jesus Christ, he doesn't sugarcoat shit. I don't know if I would've ripped the bandage off that quickly. I kinda beat around the bush.

Prescott stumbles backward, throwing his hand back against the wall. Jinx reaches out to grab his other arm, so he doesn't fall.

"Dad!"

Atticus leaps from the couch, rushing to his side before Ashton or I can reach him.

"Prescott, talk to us." Atticus helps lower him to the floor. "Are you having a heart attack?"

"I'm calling 9-1-1." I reach for my phone.

Prescott waves his hand. "I'm fine."

"Promise?" Jinx's voice cracks with worry.

Her dad brushes her wet hair away from her face. Her towel lays next to her, discarded from her mad rush to get to him.

"Promises are meant to be broken. I swear I'll be fine. What about you?"

"I'm fine. Or will be, I swear."

He chuckles. "Just like your old man. Stubborn. I'll do whatever I can to remove him from school. What can I do now?"

"Nothing. The thought of Cam sucking soup through a straw almost satisfies me."

He pulls her in for a hug. "I want you home this week-end for supper." He glances at all three of us. "That goes for you three, too."

Ashton's shoulders slump, Atticus' back straightens, and I prepare myself for one hell of a fight. Serena will no doubt try to start something with Jinx, especially now that she isn't getting a cent from Prescott. I wouldn't give that woman anything, either. She's a wicked woman. I don't know how the twins can stand their mother.

Prescott tells us that he'll be having a meeting first thing in the morning with the board members to discuss what went on. He's hopeful Cameron will be kicked out or suspended once they hear what he did. I swear if he shows his face again, I'll be dealing with him.

The only thing I'm worried about is the strings his grandfather has. Legacies are treated like Gods at this school. Liam is another legacy that we need to deal with. Cam might screw us over with the board members if we do fuck Liam up.

"I'm gonna head out also, Jinx. If you need anything, call me."

She turns to me, wet hair drying in messy waves. I slowly reach out, my hand cupping her cheek. I stroke her neck with my thumb, feeling her pulse when I rest under her chin. I press my thumb into her chin, tilting her head back. She grabs my wrist, digging her nails into my skin.

"Hey, it'll be alright. I'm sure one of the twins will stay behind."

"I'm sorry, Maddox."

"You did nothing wrong. Take it easy for the rest of the day, and I'll meet you out front tomorrow." I press a gentle kiss to her lips before walking out.

The temptation to open the bottle of Jack is strong. I'm trying not to think about it but failing miserably. I push open my door and open my cupboard. I unscrew the cap with shaky hands and take an enormous gulp; the burning sensation warms my stomach.

Collapsing on the couch, the events of the day play over in my head. No matter what she says, this is all my fault. I left her alone when I should've stayed with her. Cam wouldn't have tried anything with me next to her. I take another gulp of whisky, and my body begins to buzz from the alcohol. I need to think of a way to get Liam back.

It has to be a surprise, something he doesn't see coming.

Nine

Jinx

The look on Maddox's face as he left. It left me broken. I'm more broken than I felt sitting in that office today. No matter how many times I tell Maddox, he'll never believe me that it wasn't his fault. Just like I won't believe him when he says it wasn't mine. It's all my fault, and I'm the common denominator. With each passing day, I think more about leaving this school.

Now, Dad is going to be battling with the board for me. If he doesn't win, the twins can be kicked out; they won't even be suspended. Their future is riding on a bunch of old guys. It's not fair. I should be in that room, pleading my case. But knowing Dad, he'll never let me go through the pain of telling anyone.

Even at twenty, he still treats me like his little girl. How the hell am I supposed to tell him about my stalker? It'll break his heart. I already lost one parent. I can't lose another.

I slowly make my way back to the bathroom, latching the door behind me. I don't care what Dad says. I'm going to that meeting tomorrow. I let the twins take the fall for me once.

I won't do it again.

They deserve a chance at a proper future, and I can't keep fucking it up. This is my chance to give them one. I'll tell the members where to shove their old balls if I have to. Cameron must leave this school before taking things further with another girl.

I move to the sink and stare at myself in the mirror. My hair is drying into a mess of wavy curls, almost like my life at this point—a mess.

"Jinx?" Ashton knocks and calls my name. "You doin' alright in there?"

Closing my eyes, I blow the air out of my lungs. My chest still aches when I try to take a deep breath; I might have to make a doctor's appointment for a different inhaler. I rub my chest to relieve some of the tension, but most of it isn't from my asthma. It's from what's going on every time I leave this room.

"I'm fine, Ashton. I'll be out shortly."

"That's nice. Unlock the door, or I'll break it down."

All I wanted was a moment to myself. I can't even get that. I unlock the door and swing it open.

"What?" I snap, losing all my patience.

His blue eyes grow a shade darker. "I'll let that slide. But you are not hiding in the bathroom all afternoon. Being alone after what happened isn't healthy for you or your mind. You can talk about it if you wish, but you are sitting with us."

I remember what he said earlier about being picked up off the bathroom floor. This is the second time he's found me in the bathroom. One day, he'll give up on me. I know it. There are only so many times you try to help someone before quitting. I push past him, but his hand clamps around my wrist.

"What's going on?"

"Nothing." I try to rip my arm out of his grip, only for him to tighten his hold.

He tips my chin up, searching my eyes. "Don't lie to me. I can read you like a book. What's eating you?"

Like hell, I'm telling him what I'm about to do tomorrow. He'll only try to stop me. I can only think of one thing.

"Girly things."

He narrows his eyes, thinking for a second before letting me go. "I mean it when you want to talk."

"I know. Thanks, Ash."

"Just don't do anything stupid because I'm afraid of what I might do."

Crashing a meeting with the members isn't stupid. I leave him standing by the bathroom and head into the kitchen. Edgar lets out an ear splitting squawk when he sees me. I guess I did ignore him earlier. I watch as he hobbles toward me, and I swear he glares at me.

I kneel, placing my hand out for him. "I'm sorry. You come first from now on." He rubs his head into my hand, letting out a low kraa.

"When does his splint come off?" Atticus kneels next to me with his box of treats.

I grab a few and hold them out for Edgar to take. "I think it could come off this week. He seems to be doing much better and should be outside. I've grown accustomed to him being around everyday. It'll be hard to see him leave." Edgar quickly grabs a treat, swallowing it whole, pausing a moment before catching the last one.

"I think you'll do wonderful without him. Besides, do you think he won't visit you daily for treats?" He chuckles as Edgar hobbles to the jar, trying to get another treat.

Atticus wraps his hand around my hair, tugging it twice. I look up at him, and his face is all serious.

"I wanted to kill Cameron. Never be scared to tell me what is going on. I'll never be upset with you. I need you to know that. I can tell you blame yourself for what happened. Cameron is a predator. He feeds on people's fear, Jinx. I should've done more to him last time."

Great. Everyone is blaming themselves.

"Atticus. It's not your battle. It's mine."

"That you're not fighting alone," Ashton says from behind me.

I open my mouth, but Atticus jerks his head toward Ashton. A silent message is exchanged, and my heart skips a beat when Ashton scoops me up. A small scream spills from my mouth as I fly onto the couch.

"What the fuck?" I coughed out.

Ashton shrugs. "You needed a diversion."

Atticus walks around the couch, stopping at my head. "You need to get out of that head."

Ashton sits, lifting my legs into his lap, while Atticus lifts my head into his as he sits. Ashton grabs a foot, digging his thumb into a tender spot; my toes curl, and I groan. Atticus' fingers curl into my hair, massaging my scalp. My head flops back as my body relaxes. This is a perfect distraction. My eyes slowly drift close.

My body jolts awake, and it takes my brain a while to figure out where I am. A pool of sweat lies around me in bed, and my heart is thrumming wildly. It was only a nightmare; I tell myself. I'm in my dorm, not in the office with Cameron and Liam. I grab my phone off the nightstand, checking the time—2 a.m.

I peel the blanket away and step out of bed. I move to the dresser, finding a pair of shorts and Atticus's hoodie. Then, I moved to the bathroom. I'm surprised the guys didn't fall asleep with me. I don't even know if they are still here. I doubt they would leave me alone. The space is welcoming, I'll admit. I just need them to keep it up until I go. Sneaking around isn't my best attribute.

Turning on the shower, I twist around to grab a towel and jump when I notice Ashton leaning on the doorframe. His white-blond hair stands randomly, and my eyes drift down his chest, counting each ab. I've seen him shirtless before, but something about seeing him in his boxers does something to me. I've never seen Ashton like this before. He's always been reserved.

"Little swan. Did you have a nightmare?"

I nod.

He pushes off the doorframe, enveloping me in his arms. His skin is warm against my cheek, and he still smells like chlorine from his last swim.

"Do you need another distraction?" he whispers into my ear. He moves his hands down my back, over my ass, with a firm squeeze to my thighs; he lifts me onto the counter.

Ashton runs his hands down my thighs to my knees, pushing my legs wide. I almost forgot how to breathe when he stepped in between them. He coils his finger around the hem of Atticus' hoodie.

"I love my brother, but I hate him for letting you wear his clothes." He pulls the hoodie over my head, leaving me exposed. "You would put Aphrodite to shame, Jinx."

"Ashton," I murmured, bowing my head.

"Don't act shy on me now." He dips my chin up with his pointer finger. "I've seen you naked before."

"Yeah, but that was before."

"This is your body. You own it; nobody else does. I know it feels like you want to peel it off and burn it. It'll take a while for those feelings to go away. Know that you aren't alone. I know exactly how it feels."

His words sent a nervous chill down my spine. Hot tears welled along my lower lash line, threatening to spill with each blink—my poor Ash. My hand shook as I reached for his face. His eyes close as he turns his face deeper into my hand.

"I'm sorry, Ashton."

"I haven't been with a woman since that night, Jinx. The thought of them touching my dick makes my skin crawl."

"Is that why you won't let me?"

He slides his hand over mine, gliding it toward his mouth. With a small kiss on my palm, he moves down his neck. My fingertips press into his pulse, never feeling it skip a beat. He continues his journey, moving our hands over his chest, down his abs, just above the waistband of his boxers; our hands stop moving, and he lets out a small, painful groan.

I push him back and hop off the counter. He eased my pain. The least I can do is ease his. I gently press my lips over his heart to remind him it's still beating and that he didn't give up. No matter what, I'll be here for him. I won't leave again. I'll fight. I place kisses down his sternum; his hand moves into my hair when I kneel. Running my finger under the waistband, I watch his head fall back.

"Jinx, I'm not sure about this."

"I'll go slow. You tell me when to stop touching you."

"Okay. I can handle that." His throat bobs when he swallows.

I lower his boxers inch by inch, and when his trimmed pubes come into view, I freeze. I press my finger along the tattoo when his body jerks forward.

"Sorry, should I stop?"

"I'm sorry. Give me a second." He drops his hand to my shoulder, inhaling deep. "I take, you found my hidden tattoo?"

I run my finger over it again, hidden. It's a secret. "Why did you get it?"

"It reminded me of you, and I needed a part of you on my body."

The little black cello stands out against his blond hair. I lean forward, grazing my lips lightly across the tattoo. Ashton sucks in a trembling breath, digging his fingers into my shoulder.

"Did you want me to stop?"

"I—Okay, go slow."

I pull his boxers down lower, getting a view of the base of his dick. I look up, watching him with a slight nod; he tells me to continue. I let his boxers drop to the floor. Running my finger down the length of his shaft, I circle his tip, massaging the precum around.

"Shit, Jinx." His hand moves into my hair, pushing me closer. "Lick it."

I wrap my hand around the thickness of his shaft, bringing the tip of his dick to my lips—the velvety skin brushes against my warm lips, darting my tongue out. I taste the precum that's building.

"More," he rasps.

I lick from base to tip, his hand tightening in my hair when I bring him into my mouth. I sit there without moving, tasting him on my tongue. When I peer up, he fixes me with a wary stare. I go to pull him out, but he holds my head still.

"Just let me." He closes his eyes. "I need a second." After a long minute, he moves my head up and down at the pace he needs to go. I'll do what he needs to feel comfortable again.

"Jinx, I'm coming." Ashton moans. With a jerk of his hips forward, he spills down my throat. "Get up here. Let me taste it myself."

I straighten up, and he seizes my lips in a heartbeat. Pulling me tighter into his body, our lips move as if we're starving. When he finally pulls away, he licks his lips and smirks.

"The next time, I wanna taste us both together. Get in the shower; you're wasting water."

"Are you joining me?"

"Jinx, I need to start slow, and you being half-naked is killing me. I want you so bad, but I can't get in that shower with you."

"I get it. Go back to bed. Thanks for the distraction." I backed up, giving him space. He pulls his boxers up and turns for the door.

"You gonna be okay?" He glances over his shoulder.

I wave him off. "Yeah. I'll see you in the morning." I watch him leave, heading back to the living room area. I'm not even in the mood for a shower.

I turn the water off and change into new clothes. I have to be up in a few hours.

Ten

Jinx

I lie awake until the sun starts to peak above the trees. If I'm gonna get out of my dorm, it has to be now. I quickly get out of bed and find my most professional items in my closet. A long-sleeved A-line black dress that ends at my shins. And pair it with a thin black belt around the waist. I found my black Mary Jane platforms from the shoe rack to finish my outfit. Yeah, this look should do it. I'll be dominating that meeting like it's nothing. A little black eyeliner, and I'll be unstoppable.

Those men are up for a challenge; once I step into that room, I'm not leaving until Cameron is kicked out. I'll pick a fight if I have to. I don't care at this point. They need to know a predator is in their school and he's dangerous to any female.

When I leave my bedroom, Ash and Atticus are sprawled out, sleeping on the couch. With the lightest steps I can manage, I reach the door. Holding my breath, I turn the knob, throwing open the door, and I'm so glad it doesn't creak like some of the doors in the dorm. In a wink of an eye, I darted out into the hall, my heart lodged in my throat. I've never snuck out before, and holy hell, I don't see how people can do it all the time. I rush down the stairs before they realize I've left. I still have to get past the fourth floor.

Maddox can still catch me.

Being outside is a relief, a weight is almost lifted from not being caught. The only other students outside this early are those who want to torture their bodies by running. That's a no for me. Having a stalker is like walking on eggshells. I never know where he is or when he'll text me. I'm tired of always hiding or having one of the guys with me, and I want my life back.

It feels nice not being escorted. I can think without being watched and analyzed like a Google document. I want this all the time. I'll take it even if it's a little morsel of freedom.

The school is quiet when I step inside, somewhat eerie when no other students walk the halls. I wouldn't put it past being haunted—especially the basement. I've heard stories about a weird cult going on down there. Of course, nothing has ever been proven, but everyone talks about it like they exist. Even if they did exist, everyone would look the other way. This school doesn't like to talk about their secrets.

Then again, maybe some secrets shouldn't be found out.

I head to the directors' boardroom, where all the meetings occur. All the walls are painted a warm black, including the curved ceiling—a row of four cathedral windows overlooks the courtyard. I'm sure this is one of the only rooms that didn't get a complete reno when they redid the school. The floor is still the paved stone from the late 1800s. I sit next to the head seat, where Dad will sit, and wait.

Thirty minutes later, the first member walks through the door. With his head down, checking his phone, he doesn't notice me until he reaches the table. His hand hovers over the chair as his eyes latch onto mine.

"Oh, I'm sorry. I think you're in the wrong room, Miss." He peers down his nose at me.

I take him in, from his freshly pressed suit to his classily side-parted salt and pepper hair. He smells like money.

"Trust me. I belong here." I rest my hands on the table, getting comfortable, and watch his lip curl into a snarl. I can't wait to take him down, especially Cameron's grandfather. That'll be even better, prove to him that his dear little grandson isn't who he thinks he is.

He glares at me before returning to his phone.

My phone vibrates in my pack, and it's official; the guys know I'm gone. They'll destroy the campus looking for me; this meeting better start soon. Knowing Atticus, he will search this room, too. The door swings open, making me jump in my seat.

"Odette?"

Dad stands in the doorway with two other men when I face him. I spot Cameron's grandfather instantly. Cameron is the spitting image of his grandfather. I wonder if he learned all his pervy ways from him, too.

"Dean Hawthorne. I thought it would be appropriate to be at the meeting as well. There are a few things I would like to discuss also if that's okay?"

"We usually take a vote on these things," the man in the olive-green suit says with an exaggerated sigh.

"Barnaby, that's enough. She can speak. Sit."

Barnaby should be wearing a purple suit. I watch as he sits next to the other dickhole, the only one left standing is Cameron's grandfather. There's something about him that sends shivers down my back. His suit sleeve rides up his wrist, revealing a small tattoo on the inside of his wrist. Before I can get a better look, he sits.

"Prescott, can we start? I have places to be," Cameron's grandfather asks.

"Archer, that's enough. We're all here because of your grandson. Now shut up. Roan, are you ready to take notes?"

The dickhole on his phone looks at me again, Roan, I'm assuming. I've never seen any of these guys around the campus before. Where do they hide? And why hasn't Dad ever mentioned them before? These are things I should know about, too.

"Then start. What's going on with Cameron?"

A small scoff slips from me, and Dad snaps his head in my direction. I raise my chin; I'm not backing down.

Dad drops a file onto the table, gaining everyone's attention. "Cameron has been accused of assault on a student, and this wouldn't be the first time. The only difference is that this involves my daughter." He looks at Archer. "I won't let it slide this time."

A vein in Archer's neck popped out, and I swear I could see it throbbing from my side of the table.

"Are you imposing that my grandson raped your daughter?"

My insides tumbled into each other from his words. It came close in the bathroom at Cam's party, too. He's always finding me at my most vulnerable moments.

"That's exactly what I'm saying. Your grandson needs to leave school at once. The safety of all the students depends on it."

Archer lurches out of his seat, slamming his hand on the table. "How dare you!" he seethed.

"He speaks the truth. Your grandson is disgusting," I exploded, clenching my teeth hard.

Archer's dark eyes turn into balls of fire. "Let me guess. You're the slut that made my grandson fall for her. I should've known you were related to him." He points to Dad. "Playing around with Cameron's feeling like a dirty whore. You had it coming."

Dad lunged from his seat, and his right fist slammed out, connecting with Archer's jaw. Archer staggered backward, grabbing his face. Burnaby stood, but Dad raised his hand for him to stop.

"No, that piece of shit had it coming. No one talks about my daughter like that. Just because you're a legacy member doesn't give you the right to address a female like that. Show some respect. Did you want to see the evidence I have, Archer, or are you going to continue to be in denial?"

Roan hasn't said a word or moved the entire time. He looks somewhat bored. It doesn't surprise me; he never looked like he wanted to be here.

"Archer, we already know your grandson is a fucking pervert. Stop denying it." Roan says in a dull, annoyed voice.

"You all know?" I glare at Archer. "Do you know what he did to me in the office? No less in a public space, and you want to fight to keep him here."

"His legacy. That'd look bad on me if my grandson were to be kicked out of this school."

The image of Ash and Atticus beating Cam pops into my mind, and I smile. "Have you seen Cam lately?"

Archer leans over the table, getting close. "No, but I heard what your brothers did. I should be pressing charges."

I lean in. His five o'clock shadow is barely coming in; the crow's feet on the outer corner of his eyes are settling in deep. I'm gonna say they are not from laughing.

"You press charges, and I'll press charges. And I'll find every other girl he did something with on campus. Are you sure you want to drag your name through the mud?" My heart thumped wildly in my chest when his eyes lit up.

"Prescott, I underestimated your daughter." He backs away, turning to face Dad. "He's suspended for six weeks, and that's all."

Roan stands like the meeting is suddenly over. A throat punch is in his future. "If that's all, I have to leave now. The notes have been taken."

"We didn't agree," I argued back.

"All in favor of a six-week suspension?" Archer asks.

Barnaby and Roan raise their hands, and Archer smirks at me. "That would mean I won."

The room is quiet after they leave. Archer's words keep ringing in my head. In six weeks, Cameron will be back. How fair is that?

"I'm sorry, pumpkin. I'm proud of you for fighting, but Archer always gets his way."

I tilt my head back, trying not to cry. "I don't get it. Cam can be a major cuntfucker and all he gets is a slap on the wrist. What kind of example is that setting for the school?"

"Not a good one. I've tried to have a strong moral for this school, but the longer we stay open, the worse it seems to get. The members don't care who is accepted anymore. They want to turn it into a non-exclusive school. I'm at my wit's end, Odette."

"How come you've never mentioned this before? We could've figured something out."

Dad runs his hand through his graying hair. "There are some things you don't need to worry about. And how this school runs is one thing you shouldn't be thinking about. Now, let's get you to class."

I forgot all about classes; being in this meeting felt like I was stuck in another world. I'm scared to look at my phone, and the guys are not going to let me get away with any of this.

"Dad, can you walk me to class?"

"I would love to. Don't forget dinner at the house to-morrow. Serena is planning some big dinner party now."

"You mean a torture session. I'm only going because it's you who's asking."

He chuckles before opening the door and putting the Dean mask back on. It's the one thing I admire about him: he can hide his personal life so well at work.

And I've been a struggling mess since the start of school.

Eleven

Ashton

It took me hours to fall asleep after finding Jinx in the bathroom. I kept overplaying everything she did and how I broke my walls for her. I've only wanted her. It should've been her the first time, not some random chick at a party that took advantage of me. I'll never forgive myself for lowering my guard at a party.

I lie awake on the couch as Ace snores like nothing bothers him. I'm tempted to give the fucker a kick and wake him up. But he hardly sleeps, and I know he needs this, but something in my mind flashes with a warning. I get up and see Edgar hopping around near the front door.

"What's the matter, my man?"

"Kraa, kraa."

"Come on, let's get you back into bed. Jinx wouldn't like you getting yourself into a hissy for nothing."

I lean down and pick him up, and I swear he glares at me like I did something wrong. For a bird, he has some attitude on him, and it's no wonder he and Jinx get along so well. They are made for each other. I drop him off in his box and head for Jinx's bedroom. The first thing I noticed was that the room was quiet. She's always up before us.

"Jinx?" I call out, heading toward her bed. I reach for her blanket but stop short. I swing around, facing the bathroom, but it's empty.

I race back into the main area, kicking Ace awake. He jolts up, arms swinging, looking for somebody to hit.

His eyes meet mine. "What's going on?" He demands.

"Jinx is missing. That's what's going on. Did Maddox take her to school?" I dart around the room, trying to find my phone. This isn't like her; she always tells us the plan.

"I sent her a text. Anything from Maddox?"

I wave my phone at him. "Dude, I just found my phone." I shoot Maddox a brief message without freaking him out.

"Where could she have gone? She knows not to leave without one of us." His voice shook with fury, and I feel sorry for whoever steps in his way today.

I pace her small kitchen, thinking of all the places she could have gone. Yesterday was tiresome for her, so I don't blame her for escaping.

"She hasn't replied, what about Maddox?" He looks at me with desperation in his eyes.

I slowly shake my head. I have no idea where Maddox or Jinx are. I don't want to think of all the possibilities, or I'll start falling apart. "I'm gonna run down to Maddox's place and see if he's there. Call Spencer. Maybe he knows."

I fling open the door and bolt down the hall. My heart pounds beneath my rib cage as I fly down the stairs. Why can't this place have an elevator? What if her stalker caught up with her? Would she have met him without us? No, I don't think she would've; at least, I don't think she would.

I bang on Maddox's door loud enough to wake the entire floor. "Maddox, come on, man. Wake up." I enter his door code and slip into another disaster. I should've known he would self-destruct when he left last night. One of us should've gone with him.

The sight of him lying on the couch breaks my heart, and a bottle of Jack sits on the table, empty. I inch closer, watching his chest rise. I release a tight breath, knowing today isn't the day I lose my best friend.

"Maddox, I swear you will kill me one day," I whisper.

I clamp my hand on his shoulder, shaking him awake. He extended a hand, and I blocked it before he could punch me in the face. "M, it's me. Ash. You're safe."

I hold his hand, and his eyes grow distant as if he is seeing things from the past. The things he went through growing up don't naturally go away when you get older. I should've known to wake him gentler. His eyes search mine while he comes back.

"Ash?" he croaked.

I squeeze his hand. "Yeah, man, it's me."

"I fucked up again." His eyelids drift closed. "I'm sorry, I let everyone down. I shouldn't be here."

"Maddox, you didn't let anyone down. We had no idea that would happen, and you aren't a fortune teller. You can't always blame yourself when things go wrong."

He opens his eyes. "I'm cursed, Ash. You should know this by now."

"You aren't. If that were true, you wouldn't have Atticus, nor would I still. Now come on, we have trouble in paradise."

He slowly pulls himself up with a groan, and that hangover is going to be a killer today. And once I tell him about Jinx, he's going to lose his shit.

"What's going on?" He pushes his fingers through his brunette hair.

I bite down on my lower lip, trying to figure out the best way to deliver this news. Rip it off like a Band-Aid. "Jinx is missing; she's not answering her phone, and she never left a clue where she would've gone."

His head snaps up. "She never mentioned anything to me. Have you called her dad?" His eyes darted across my face.

I didn't even think about calling Prescott, but do I want to get him worried? She couldn't leave the school grounds unless she found a ride from somebody else. But that would be a last resort—I hope.

"Her dad doesn't know anything that's happening with her stalker friend, and I don't want to be the one to drop that news."

"You think this has something to do with *Unknown*?"

I pick the bottle of Jack up and walk to the kitchen sink. "Fuck, I don't know. I'm trying to think of all the possibilities and praying that it isn't the one."

"I'll change, and then we can head out."

Me: Any news?

I hate not knowing anything, and Ace is shitty at updates. He better have called Spencer.

Ace: Nothing. Did she have an early class that we didn't know about?

Me: I don't think so. She usually tells us everything.

Ace: I say we check the school; she has to be there.

Me: I'll meet you outside in 10

As I wait for Maddox, I do a quick clean-up. He doesn't need to live in this mess. I wish there were more I could do for him. Until he is ready, all I can do is show my support.

When we walk out of the dorm, Atticus is sitting on the bench waiting for us. When he notices us, he nods his head solemnly, getting up and walking away. I feel bad for him as well. He finally got Jinx back, and now she's missing. I can't imagine what's running through his head.

Maddox and I take off after him, heading for the main building. You can't overlook a tiny chick in all-black. I tried calling her again, only for it to ring and go to voicemail. She's making this worse for herself. I already feel bad once Atticus gets ahold of her. Or when we all get our hands on her, the punishment will break her.

Students are milling around the front entrance, whispering to each other. When they see us, they back away, growing quiet. We're dicks, but not that big of ones. Entering the school, the silence only follows. The hair on the back of my neck lifts the further we move; I tuck my hands into my jean pockets, flexing my fingers against my thigh as I walk.

"Why is everyone so quiet?" Maddox addresses.

"Fuck if I know, but it's pissing me off." Atticus glares at a couple hanging around the office. They make no attempt to move.

Whatever happened, the news traveled fast. What I don't understand is why we don't know yet. Does this have something to do with Cam? If so, then the Coach should've told us something by now. I don't like this at all.

"We need to talk to Prescott now." I don't wait for them to follow.

Florence is typing away and doesn't hear me enter. Today, she's wearing a pinstripe suit with a white shirt, and I must say it's giving me Beetle Juice vibes. I tap the desk, and she smiles with delight at me.

"Good morning. Prescott isn't in yet. You can wait out here if you wish." She points to the seat behind me.

"That's alright. Do you know where he is by chance?"

"He had a morning meeting in the boardroom. I do believe the meeting is over."

I turn toward the guys to see what they want to do. I have to hold myself back from knocking on every class door to find her. Maddox pulls his phone out, a last-ditch attempt. With a roll of his eyes, he places his phone back in his pocket.

"Florence, can you find out what class Odette has?" Ace inquired.

"I can. Is something the matter?"

"No, she just forgot something, and I can't remember which class she said she would be in."

Florence types away, and my body tingles with anticipation. This will only work if she's in a class. If not, I have no idea where to look. I feel completely useless.

"It says she's in Musicology. Do you know where that is?" Her eyes lifted to meet mine. "I wouldn't interrupt her if she's in there. You all know how much music is significant to her."

"Yeah, thanks, Florence."

She's right, no matter how much we're pissed at her. We can't fuck with her career, she needs it to get out of this shitty town, and I hope Atticus can see the same picture I can.

"Now what?" I ask.

"We head to her class. I don't give a shit. I need to know she's there."

Never mind, he doesn't give a shit.

Twelve

Atticus

The things I'm going to do when I get my hands on Jinx. She'll wish she was in another State. Anything could've happened to her. For all I know, she isn't even in this class. And if one more fucking prick stares at me when I walk the halls, I'm going to punch the shit out of them.

"Why won't one of these sad sacks of shit just tell us what's going on?"

"My guess is they're all chicken shits." Maddox shook his head in disbelief.

Chicken shits is putting it nicely.

"Don't pay them attention, Ace. Jinx is our priority at the moment," Ash reminds me.

It's easy for him to say he's the calm one. This is making me go insane. If Jinx thinks she's getting out of my sight for one second, she's dead wrong. I'll handcuff her to myself if need be. This wasn't how I expected today to start. What the fuck was she thinking, leaving the dorm without us? She knows anything can happen to her. Does she not care?

The sound of fighting pulled me from my thoughts. Maddox has a jackass held up against the brick wall. A circle of onlookers began to grow. The only thing saving us is we can't get expelled.

"Maddox? What's going on?" I grip him by the shoulder without taking his attention away from the jackass.

Maddox slams the jackass further into the wall when he starts fighting back. "This prick was talking shit about you, and Ashton and I had had enough. I'm sure he would like to repeat a few things, would you?"

He lets out a low chuckle. "Fuck you. You come into this school acting like the top dog, but you aren't. You're fucking nothing. You just proved that today."

I hate when people beat around the bush. Tell it how it is. It isn't that hard. Maddox must not like that answer either. His fist moves fast, connecting with the jackass's nose. Blood pours in a steady stream down his mouth and onto his shirt.

"Now speak, or I'll make you bleed someplace else." Maddox jerks forward.

Jackass cowers, covering his face. "Fine. It's because of those dickheads that Cam got suspended from school."

"Their fault because?" Maddox urges him to continue.

"They beat the shit out of him because of their sister. She asked for it, and Cam still got the blame for everything."

I swing my arm out, stopping Ashton. "Don't. I know who started this rumor, and he's next on the list and owes you one, brother." I fixed the jackass with a cruel stare. I hope he tells Liam we're after him.

I back away, catching a glimpse of our girl in the crowd.

"Run." I mouthed.

Panic stirred behind her eyes as she watched me weave amongst the crowd, my pulse skyrocketing to my fingertips with every step. She spins on her heels, taking off for the doors, kicking my heart into gear.

The chase is on.

I know exactly where she's running to, back to the dorms. That's not where I want to have fun. I take the path that leads behind the dorm, and my mind races with the thought of her begging me to let her go. But that isn't happening, not until she learns her lesson. I open the back door, running past the student lounge and basement entrance. Pushing through the front door, I stop as she's rounding the corner.

Her body skids to a stop, and she's heaving a chest full of air through her mouth. I take a step forward and watch as she moves backward.

"Little grim. Have you had enough?"

"No," she said, catching her breath.

I softly laughed. "You should run then, but if I catch you. I'm fucking you no matter where you are."

I spot Ashton and Maddox coming up behind her, and I give them a nod toward the art studio. No matter how much I want her in public, that won't happen, not with her stalker somewhere. Jinx slowly turns around, facing the guys.

"You two are in on this?" Her lips trembled as she realized she didn't have anyone to turn to.

"Yeah, baby. You gave us one hell of a scare."

She swung around and pelted down the path, heading in the direction I needed.

"Time to catch my prey. Meet you in the furthest art room." I break into a run, trying to cut her off before she can change directions. She can't run forever, the less fight in her, the better. I catch the scent of her coconut perfume; the closer I get, my dick thickens. I watch her round the corner of the art building.

She's bent over when I round the corner, catching her breath, and doesn't see me coming. I wrap my arms around her waist, lifting her in the air. She lets out a scream and wiggles in my hold.

"Do you want me to drop you?" I move her closer to my chest.

She grunts. "I want you to leave me alone."

I move toward the wall, slamming her against it, and wrap her legs around my hips. My fingers dig into her thighs. I drop my lips to her neck, feeling her pulse hammer. "Jinx, I'll never leave you alone. Haven't you figured that out yet?"

"I hate you!" she screamed savagely. She fights against my hold, but I press her further into the wall.

"Fight me. I love it." I move her dress up her thighs, exposing her black thong. She squirms when I run my finger over her covered clit. "What's the matter, little grim? Getting wet at the thought of someone watching?"

Her gaze dips down to my lips. No matter how much she says she hates me, I know differently. I move her thong to the side and run my fingers lightly over her clit. Her eyes fall close, and she drops her head against the wall.

"Tell me what you want, little grim." I move my fingers lower, sliding them into her wet entrance. She cries out, digging her nails into my shoulder and arching into my fingers. I look around and ensure we are alone; the last thing I need is for the *Unknown* to find her.

"Atticus, we can't," she whispered, her eyes smoldering with lust.

"We can and we will." I withdraw my fingers and undo my jeans. I reposition her lower on my hips, feeling the warmth of her pussy on my dick. "Fuckin, scream. Let him know who you belong to." I slam into her, stretching her. Her lovely scream vibrates in my ear as her fingers weave into my hair and pull tight. My dick throbs from the pain, making me thrust deeper until our hips meet.

She tries to push me away with her other hand, but there's no point. It only makes me want her more. Holding her up with one hand, I slide my other hand around her slender neck; with a slight clench, I restrict her breathing. She bucks her hips, driving herself further on my dick.

"Fuck, yes," I grunt when her pussy tightens around me. "I'm gonna make you nice and wet for Maddox, little grim." Rubbing my thumb against her pulsing vein, I squeeze her neck a little harder and watch her eyes close. I feel her swallow against my palm, rocking faster. The pleasure came out of nowhere.

"Jinx, you're mine," I tell her as I spill deep inside of her. I remove my hand from her neck and admire the red mark that I made. I drop her legs and catch her when she falls forward. "I got you. I'll never let you go. No one will ever take you away from me."

"I still hate you," she mumbles against my chest.

"Hate turns into love, little grim." I grab her hand, leading her into the art building. I have no idea what the guys have set up. I gave them enough time to be ready.

I hate being in this stupid building. Taking an art class shouldn't even be on my class list. I can't even paint a stick person. Ash is the artist, the swimmer, and the captivating person of the family. No matter what he thinks, he's not a quitter like I am.

The room I told the guys to meet me in is dimly lit when we approach, and I feel Jinx slowing down. Giving her a hard tug across the doorway, I slam the door behind us and watch Ash and Mad prowl toward Jinx, never taking their eyes off her.

"Little swan, did you have fun with my brother?"

She crosses her arms and huffs. "I wouldn't call that fun," her voice comes out raspy.

Maddox gives her a knowing smirk. "He didn't get you off, did he, baby." He walks behind her, running his finger slowly up her arm, stopping at the top of her shoulder. "Do you need to feel something?"

I watch as Jinx drops her head to her chest.

"Don't be shy, little swan. You have to tell us what you need, or you won't get anything." Ashton stands toe to toe but never touches her.

"I want to come." Her cheeks grew faintly pink.

Ashton tips her chin up, staring into her green eyes. "How?"

Maddox runs his finger down the middle of her back, and I watch as she shivers from his touch. Usually, Ash is the one who watches, but now I can see why he does. I can't put words to describe the intimacy between the three of them. Watching Jinx lose herself from a simple touch is a treasure.

"I know you aren't ready, but I'm sure you have something planned," she told him genuinely, knowing his limits.

He leans in, placing his lips so tenderly on hers. I haven't seen him close to anyone since that night at the college party. I should've been there for him; I'll never forgive myself.

Thirteen

Jinx

My brain is working on its last cell, and I can't get enough air into my lungs. These boys are trying to kill me—my hand trembles when I reach for Ashton's shirt, pulling him closer. He works his lips across my jaw, and Maddox wraps his arms around my waist, working to undo my belt; drawing a deep breath, I try to fill my lungs with air. With them this close is like having a vacuum; they keep sucking all the air from me.

"I'm gonna make you beg, baby," Maddox whispers next to my ear.

Ashton moves back, pulling his shirt over his head, and I admire what swimming has done to his body over the years.

"See something you like?" He rubs his hand along his abs.

I roll my eyes. "Just that ego of yours needs to have a seat, Ashton." Maddox chuckles, rocking our bodies.

Atticus laughs from behind us, and I won't lie, I kinda forgot that he was here.

"What state did Atticus leave you in?" Maddox asks as he drags my dress up past my hips. The cool air hits my wet thong, sending a shiver down my thighs. Maddox lets out a slight smirk. "Guess I don't need to check." He pulls the rest of my dress over my head with a long tug.

I stand before all three, wearing only my black bralette, thong, and Mary Janes. I've never felt so unsexy in my life. The one day that I chose not to wear fishnets or sexier shoes.

"So beautiful," I hear Ashton say. "Get on the floor for me."

I carefully go to where Ash laid down the giant canvas drop cloth; he takes my hand and helps me to my knees.

"Just how I like you." He brushes my hair away from my face, tilting my chin upward. His pale blue eyes pierce into me, digging into the depths of my soul. If he looks deep enough, he'll be able to find all my flaws. "Maddox, get over here, she's ready for you."

I watch Maddox appear from the corner of my eye, unzipping his jeans as he walks. My pussy throbs when he pulls his dick out, and Ashton turns my head to face it. With a lick of my lips, Maddox moves forward, lifting his dick to my wet lips.

"Open for me."

My jaw drops fast, and I grab the back of Maddox's thighs, bringing him closer. With a couple of smacks against my lips, he shoves his dick into my mouth, digging my nails into his skin when he reaches the back of my throat.

"God, baby. I love it when you take it all." He groans, pulling out halfway before slowly pushing back in.

I take a deep breath through my nose and open my mouth wider. Spit falls from the corner of my mouth onto my chest with each thrust. I gag when he drives too far back.

"So perfect," Ashton says, adjusting himself. "Maddox lay down. Jinx, you're going to ride him."

Maddox removes his jeans and hoodie before doing what Ashton says. He curls his index finger towards his palm in a come here gesture. I go to stand, but he shakes his head. "On your knees, crawl to me, Jinx." One thing about Maddox is that he isn't scared to tell you what to do.

The floor digs into my knees as I make my way to Maddox. When I reach Maddox's side, Ashton walks behind me, running his hand down my back. He hooks his finger into my thong, dragging it down my thighs. I lift each knee and watch him toss it to the side. His hand grips my calf before sliding back up my leg.

"This ass of yours, Jinx." His hand lands hard on my right cheek with a sharp snap. "I'm going to have fun breaking it in."

I drop my head onto Maddox's thigh when I think of everything Ashton could do to me. A hand tangled in my hair, pulling my head upward, and my eyes clash with a pair of hazel ones. He doesn't stop pulling my hair until I'm on top of him; spreading my legs, I straddle him.

"Fuck, I can feel how wet you are."

I rub my pussy against his dick. "That's Atticus's cum. He wanted me ready for you." Maddox shifts his gaze to Atticus.

"I owe you one." He lifts me and slams me down on his hardness. Before I can scream, Ashton covers my mouth.

"We're in school, little swan. Keep it down." He moves his hand, waiting for my answer.

I close my eyes, nodding as Maddox flexes his hips. "I'll try." I let out a silent moan the more Maddox moved; the butterflies danced in my skin, bringing me closer and closer to exploding. I turn my head, getting a view of Atticus. He leaned against the counter, arms crossed over his chest, taking us in with caution. He hasn't taken his eyes off me once, and when I feel my orgasm coming,

I still watch him. I watch the side of his jaw tick because it's Maddox making me come and not him.

"Jesus, Jinx. Does watching another man make you come that hard?" Maddox traces his fingertip along my jaw, bringing my attention back to him.

A smile ran along my lips. "I like payback."

"Naughty girl. I like it." Maddox chuckles.

I slowly rock my hips, using his pelvic bone to rub my clit. My head spins from the sensation, and I dig my nails into his chest as I get closer, and he groans from the pain. Something cold and wet hits my ass crack, then Ashton presses gentle kisses along my back.

"Shh, little swan. Enjoy it." He smacks me with something hard before running it between my ass cheeks. "Breathe out and relax for me. I'll take it slow."

Maddox wraps his arms around me, bringing me closer to his chest and placing a kiss on my neck. "Did you want to watch?"

I turn my head and see Ashton holding an artist's paintbrush with a thick, tapered handle, and he's applying lube to it. I was not expecting this, but we're talking about Ashton. He's obsessed with object insertion.

He gave me a trusted gaze, inhaling courage—I gave him a slight nod.

Maddox rubs my back as Ashton moves the paintbrush to my asshole. He slowly pushes the handle in, and I hold my breath.

"Breath, baby," Maddox whispers. "We won't hurt you. Tell us if it's too much, and we'll stop."

Ashton pushes the handle in and out, fire and euphoria charged throughout my veins. I've never felt so many sensations going on at the same time. Maddox moves his hips at a slow pace, and I lose my breath.

"You're doing so well, Jinx," Ashton reassures me.

Yeah, I can feel it. I'm not sure who to focus on because the motion from either of them is too much. I jolt forward, soaking Maddox as my orgasm washes over me. I drop my face into his neck, moaning when Ashton keeps pumping the paintbrush, working another orgasm from me. He drops the paintbrush next to Maddox and me and steps back with a dazed look. It's like he's content with himself, and that's all he needs.

"I'm not done yet, baby." Maddox slides me back onto his dick, and we both groan when he thrusts deep.

I've lost count of how many times I've come so far, and I'm not sure it's possible to have any more. My body is emotionally spent.

"Just one more, and then you're done. Finish with me." He holds me closer to his chest and pounds into me fast. Slamming my eyes closed, I bite his neck as I come. "Jinx, fuck." His fingers grip my waist tightly as he slams once more into me.

I lie still on top of him, and my chest tightens with each breath I try to take. Maddox rolls me on my back, and I hear a rustling in the background. I try to sit up, only to end up coughing.

"Don't. Atticus is trying to find your inhaler."

Tears pool in the corner of my eyes the more I struggle to breathe. I glimpse at Maddox, and his face is rumpled with something haunting. The more I try to draw air into my lungs, the more my chest aches.

"Here, exhale and open." Atticus shoves my inhaler in my face. Inhaling that dry powder always relaxes my mind, but I'm exhausted.

"Come on, baby, I'll get you dressed, and we'll get you back to your room."

I give him a sleepy gaze. "I can get there by myself."

"Don't be stupid, Jinx. You still have a stalker out there, and you can hardly hold your head up," Atticus barked back.

"Don't be so stubborn, Jinx." Aston holds my bra out for me. I grab it and my dress.

So much for getting a smidge of independence, it was nice while it lasted, but now my babysitters won't let me see an inch of freedom again. I should've told Dad about *Unknown* this morning when he walked me to class. As much as I would hate telling him, maybe he could've offered help. I can't keep living like this.

I jump when warm fingers stroke my cheek, pulling me out of my thoughts.

"Penny for your thoughts?" Atticus asks, taking a seat next to me.

I pull my knees to my chest and wrap my dress over them. I watch Maddox and Ashton clean the room before turning to Atticus.

"I think I might tell Dad about the stalker."

"What do you think he'll do?"

I shrug. How am I supposed to know? It could go two ways: him dragging me out of this school or bringing in security.

"I guess we'll see when we visit tomorrow for supper. Figured it would be best to do it while we aren't at school."

He quirked a pale brow at me. "You better make sure Mother isn't around when you tell him."

Fuckin' Serena. She's been pissed with me ever since I told her she doesn't get anything from Dad and that the school belongs to him. I haven't been back to the house since.

Now, I have no choice but to show up.

Fourteen

Jinx

The only thing I want more in life is to sleep in on a Saturday and hang out with Spence. I feel like I haven't seen him in ages, and I miss my bestie. I've been the world's worst friend, yet he still won't make the first move. He'll make me come crawling to him because, let's face it, it's all my fault for ignoring him. I haven't even watched one of his streams in a week. Some supportive friend.

I haven't said much since last night, and the guys never asked about the meeting. Honestly, I'm glad. If they knew what Cam's grandfather is like, they probably would lose their shit all over again. And you can't touch legacy status here. I'm trying to figure out how to tell Dad about my little unwanted friend, and luckily for us, Serena wants us to show up early for dinner. So now I'm stuck in the back seat of Maddox's Impala heading into Grovedale.

I can already tell how this supper is going to go. Serena will act all holy for the first hour, but as soon as the food hits the table, she'll start in on everyone. She'll complain about how we don't love her or that nobody has time for her. She is like a broken record.

I hate coming back to this house.

"How long do you think it'll take Mom to blow her top?" Ashton laughs from the seat next to me.

"With how Jinx talked to her last time, not very long. I'm just curious why she wanted us to show up early," Atticus replies.

Maddox just shakes his head but continues to drive. I stay quiet, too, because the twins are right. We won't hear quiet once we step foot into that house again. I stare out the car window, watching the trees pass by. I used to enjoy watching the scenery pass by, but now it's like watching time slowly drift away. Sooner or later, everything we know will just disappear.

The street I grew up on hasn't changed at all. Every house has a pristine lawn, and brick pillars stand on either side of the driveway. The only thing that makes Dad's house stand out is the little flower bed he planted in the front. The HOA had a huge hissy fit over it, but in the end, Dad won.

Maddox pulls into the driveway and my heart races. Dinner, and then we can leave. I'm not staying here longer than we have, too. I'll eat, tell Dad what I need, and try to ignore all the rude comments that are gonna spill from Serena's fat, fake lips.

"Are you ready because it's going to be a long-ass night?" Maddox asks, putting the car into park.

"Yeah, let's get this over with." Ashton opens the door, stepping out first.

I wait until the guys exit before leaving, trying to find my nerves, but I think I left them under my pillow.

"Move it, Odette." Atticus holds my door open.

I shoot him a glare. "Don't use my full name." I shove him aside and storm to the front door. I reach for the door handle and freeze.

"You got this, baby. One deep breath." Maddox cradles his hand around mine, pressing his chest against my back. I feel him take a deep breath in, and I mimic him. "Ready?"

"No."

"Perfect, let's go." He pushes the door open, and we're greeted with the scent of roast turkey.

Maddox groans beside me, and I know I lost him to a meal. Who cooks a turkey for a small get-together? The further we step into the house, the more things unfold. The living room has guests I've never seen before. I turn to Ashton, and his eyebrows snap together as he shrugs.

"Mother, what the fuck is all this?" Atticus doesn't hold back. You can always leave it to him to find some answers.

Serena dramatically places her hand on her chest. With a loud inhale. "Atticus Banks, you shall not speak like that in front of our guests. Show some manners."

"Show some respect," I mumble under my breath.

Serena's head quickly snaps in my direction, reminding me of a creepy doll. "Watch your mouth, you ungrateful child." Her lip curls in a snarl, and I secretly wish it would stay like that.

Maddox grips my shoulder, steering me into the kitchen before I can say anything back. It was a wise choice because what I have to say probably wouldn't end in either of our favor. And I promised Dad I would be on my best behavior.

"You have to calm yourself, baby. You can't anger the beast all the time."

"I can if she's being a cuntwaffle, Maddox. She does it purposefully, and I'll bring her down one day."

I felt his arms slide around my waist and chin resting on my head—I hate being short sometimes.

"The ill wishes of others can be the downfall of the empire. Be careful."

I tilt my head back, forcing him to move his head until I feel his lips next to mine. "Such wise words," I say quietly. His hand wraps around my hair, holding me still as he presses his lips to mine. An upside-down kiss is my new favorite thing in the world.

"That's enough, kids. Break it up," Dad grumbles. "There are some things a father doesn't want to see, and I'm not ready for this."

Maddox smiles against my lips before standing me up. "Behave, or I'll reenact my teenage fantasy later," he whispers before walking away.

I let out a nervous laugh before turning to Dad. "What's up with all the people out there?" I point to the living room.

He waves me off. "She's joining something, I can't recall. It doesn't matter what I say. Serena will do what she wants."

"That isn't fair to you, Dad. Why are you still with her?" I watch as he preps the vegetables, and his face falls.

"I don't want to live the rest of my life alone. And if I have to keep what little company I can, I will."

I can feel my heart drop to my feet. This entire time, Dad could have found someone he cared for instead of settling for what he thought he deserved. Hearing Serena's banshee laugh from the next room makes my skin crawl. Knowing what she's doing to my dad is making me go insane.

"Pumpkin. What's going on in that brain of yours?"

"Nothing, don't worry about me."

He narrows his eyes but continues to cut his vegetables. At least I didn't say I was fine, and if I weren't such a coward, this would've been the perfect chance to tell him about my little stalker problem. But every time I want to say it, my throat dries up.

It's also weird that I haven't heard from *Unknown*. He's usually up my butt, maybe he's found another victim—wishful thinking.

"And if you follow me, my amazing husband is cooking us dinner," Serena's voice grows louder.

The hairs on my neck slowly stand when Roan walks in last. The dickhole from the meeting. Why didn't Dad mention that he was entertaining a legacy asshole? Roan's mouth jerks into a grin as he walks past me, never looking at me.

"Find a seat around the table; don't be scared who you sit by," Serena continues to talk.

The table quickly fills, and I watch everyone sit, leaving one seat open. Atticus grips the back of the empty chair, waiting for me. It's not him I'm worried about. Taking my time, I move toward the table and pull the chair out. My shoulder brushes his when I sit, and my body stiffens.

"What's the matter, Odette? Still pissed about yesterday?"

I tilt my head and meet his eyes. "No, Roan. Because in the end I won. You can throw around all the power in the world, but it doesn't mean dickshit in the end."

Atticus leans in, keeping his voice low, "What's this about?"

"Cameron."

Ashton and Maddox both glare at me from across the table. I almost feel guilty for not telling them about the meeting. Then again, they didn't ask for details. Before they can bitch me out, Dad saves me.

"Turkey is ready. Make room." He set down the platter, and my stomach rumbled.

"Hungry, Odette?" Roan nudges me.

If he touches me again, my fork will go through his hand. How the hell does he and Serena know each other? I risk a glance at Serena, and she leans back in her seat, tilts her head, and shoots me a smirk on her overly lined lips.

"Ashton, hunny, why don't you carve the turkey?" she says without looking away from me.

Ashton groans but stands. "Yeah, I guess. Prescott, if you don't mind."

"Not at all. My old hands could use a break, son." Dad passed him the knife, and Serena's mouth carries a vile smile.

I've never trusted her, but ever since I told her she's a poor bitch I can't trust her at all. She's planning something, but what is the question? And I have no way of proving anything, especially being at school all the time. I have no one here who can check on Dad all the time. I definitely can't ask Roan; he's conspiring something with the bitch, too—I know it.

I scan the rest of the guests, and none seem familiar, but I can't trust them if they are friends of Serena's. Too many snakes are at this table, and my dad is the poor rat about to be eaten.

"I have a question," Atticus speaks up.

"Of course, my dear." Serena smiles at him.

Atticus chuckles. "Who the fuck are all these people crashing our family dinner?"

Ashton snickers under his breath as he finishes carving. "Yeah. Mom. I was hoping for a peaceful dinner of Jinx, bitching you out again."

I bite my lip, holding back a laugh.

"You watch your mouth. This is still my house, and I won't tolerate disrespect in front of my guests," she hissed darkly.

"My dad's house, actually." I remind her. I caught her fingers twitching over her knife. "Remember, you get nothing if he dies. You become the poor broke bitch you were before."

Her fingers wrap around the handle.

Fifteen

Maddox

This entire supper is heading down the drain. Serena is losing it minute by minute, and I'm trying not to add fuel to the fire. But Jinx, oh boy. She isn't holding back. It would've been fine if Serena knew how to keep her mouth shut, but she always finds a way of getting her little digs in.

"You watch your mouth, and it's still my house until the end, you little bitch." Serena stands, tipping her chair over and grabbing for the butter knife from the table.

"Serena, sit down," Prescott breathed exhaustedly.

No one speaks, and whoever is sitting next to me grabs the dish of vegetables like this doesn't faze him. For all I know, this could be normal for him. But Serena is done for. I watch Prescott gently place his fork on the edge of his plate and push his chair out. I glance at Atticus, but he's watching Prescott; as much as Ace hates his mother, he won't think twice about stopping Prescott from hurting her.

"Serena, a word in my office, please."

She screwed up her nose. "No, you can say what you want here."

His mouth drops to an unforgiving angle, and you can feel the temperature drop. I've never seen him angry in all the years of knowing him. Prescott stands and faces Serena.

"You wanted to host a dinner party for your friends, so I suggest you be a host. You aren't making a perfect impression now, are you?"

Her lips flop open; putting her in her place doesn't take much. She slowly moves her chair back to the table and sits. That image is everything when you have nothing. Ashton chuckles before shoving turkey into his mouth. There is no love loss there.

"Didn't know I was signing up for dinner and a show. This is a perfect night, hey Odette," The douche next to Jinx says, nudging her. A flash of repulse passed over her face.

I need to know who this asshole is. Douche looks a little too comfortable with her. "I'm sorry, who are you?"

"Me?" Douche points to his chest. "I'm Roan, and I work with Prescott."

I raise an eyebrow slowly. "And why are you all touchy-feely with my girlfriend?" I lower my voice.

"Odette?"

"Is there anyone else at the table that could be my girlfriend? Don't act all stupid."

"Oh, we go way back, don't we?" He looks at her and grins.

"No, we don't. We met yesterday at the meeting, and for some reason, he thinks we're friends."

Atticus wraps his arm around her shoulder, pulling her close. "Touch or talk to her again, and that will be the last thing you do."

Roan looks between Atticus and me. "I'm confused. What's going on here."

"It's not that hard to figure out, asshole. She has more than one boyfriend," Ashton adds.

Prescott coughs. Oops, guess we forgot he didn't know that the twins were dating his daughter.

"Odette? They are your brothers," Prescott spoke in a strangled voice.

"Stepbrothers, Prescott. There is no blood," Atticus says. And it's not like we grew up together."

He glances between the twins with pure shock. His whole world is crashing around him. When his eyes land on Jinx, pain fills them.

"I'm sorry, Dad," she sniffs, backing her chair away from the table, and rushes out of the dining room.

Serena scoffs. "Go figure she would go after my sons, can't keep her grabby hands to herself. Must've gotten that from her mother."

The air drains from the room; words fail me. That's one subject we never bring up, and if we did, those words in that sentence would never be a thought. I'm glad Jinx isn't here to hear them.

"Mother, I suggest you fuckin leave now," Atticus' voice turns icy.

Prescott hadn't moved; his face turning dark with anger. Staring forward, he says. "You have half an hour to gather your things and get out of my house before things get out of hand."

"You can't do this," she shrieked.

"I can, and I did. You will never speak about my daughter or my wife like that."

"I'm your wife," she spits out.

"No, Serena. You most definitely are not." He finally looks at her. "You are nothing. Dinner is over. Everyone get out of my house."

I watch everyone leave, minus Roan.

"Come, Serena, I'll help you." Roan stands holding his hand out. Well, if this doesn't seal the fuckin deal on why Roan is here—he's sleeping with Serena.

When I enter the living room, I find Jinx curled up on the couch, wrapped in a blanket, staring out the window. She doesn't flinch when I bury my hand into her hair and kiss her forehead.

"Baby, your dad doesn't hate or think less of you. Give him some time. It was a lot to take in."

She bowed her head slightly. "I know. I didn't expect a table full of strangers to know my love life. It's embarrassing."

"Yeah, I know it is," I answered with a soft laugh. "I think we all do now."

"Can we leave yet?"

Apparently, she has no clue what went down, and I'm not about to tell her what Serena said about her mother. That's one fight I'm not about to start. I think Prescott handled it the best he could, but I would've laid her out on the floor. Woman or not, I would've hit her.

"Maybe talk to your dad first."

"Worst dinner ever." She groans.

"I don't know, it was entertaining like always. It's never a dull moment when you and Serena go at it. I'm sure she was gonna throw that knife at you." I help her stand and drape an arm over her shoulders.

"Oh, she was for sure. That stupid cunt. But if you think about it, it explains Atticus's temper."

I pull her closer, and she wraps her arm around my waist as we walk into the kitchen, where the guys drink a beer at the island.

"Little grim, my wicked woman, you." Atticus raises his beer with a grin.

"I didn't do anything," she says, confused.

Ashton chuckles in his beer can. Bringing it away from his mouth, he says, "You damn near finished your father's marriage. I think that's a win for you."

Jinx climbs on the bar stool next to Ashton, stealing his beer. "I don't know what you guys mean." Taking a long drink, she squeezes the empty can and drops it on the countertop. "All I did was tell her the truth yet again and somehow expose our relationship."

"Boys, can I have the room, please? I need a word with my daughter."

Without a word, we leave for the backyard. It's a little chilly outside, but it feels welcoming, especially after all that shit.

"Think she'll be okay in there?" Ashton asks, sitting on the step.

I lean on the rail, looking over the yard. I spent much time out here when the twins first moved it; it was peaceful then.

"I'm sure she'll be alright. She has a lot to tell her dad." I turn, taking in his features. He still looks like the same punk ass kid when I first met him, unlike his brother, the troublemaker.

"She better tell him about her fuckin' stalker, or I will. It's bullshit that he doesn't know. His school has issues, and he needs to deal with them." Atticus stalks across the yard, digging into his pants pocket and putting a joint to his lips.

Ashton turns slightly, looking up at me. "He's right, you know. Jinx should've told him from the start, or one of us should have."

"Jinx works through things on her own. We all know this, and telling her how to do things never goes as planned. We can only hope she tells him tonight before things escalate."

Even as the words leave my mouth, they don't mean anything. Jinx won't tell her dad anything. Stubborn doesn't even begin to describe her. Once she set her mind on something, good luck changing it; she didn't think twice about leaving this town or the ones in it behind. Not once returning for a visit, she was dead set on forgetting us all.

It's hard to look past that. If Jinx could do it once, what's to say she won't do it again? I want to trust her, but something in the back of my mind keeps telling me not to. And I understand it's unfair to think those things, but

I also trusted my parents, who did precisely the same thing.

They were never there for me. I was used to the lies, but deep down, I believed them when they told me they would stop drinking and the drugs. Then that escalated to cutting me down when they didn't get their fix quickly enough. It was my fault, and I was the useless child that ruined everything good in their life. If not for me, they would be living on top of the world. Now, I couldn't care less where they are; burning the house down never did relieve me of anything. How does one heal a fucked-up heart? Can it even be healed?

"What's wrong?" Ashton snaps his fingers, grabbing my attention.

I give my head a shake. "Nothing, unwanted thoughts is all."

"Don't let them define you; you are stronger than you think you are, Maddox. If they wanted to be parents, they would've been. They chose their path, and it will never be your fault."

"Yeah. I just don't believe it, that's all."

His face crinkled with concern. "Maddox. You have us remember."

Until I don't, then what? I'm so dead inside that I'm afraid I won't feel much of anything soon, not even love.

Sixteen

Atticus

It's been two days since the disaster dinner. Jinx has been out of sorts since her talk with Prescott. Even when we asked what they talked about, she wouldn't tell us about it. She told us not to worry about it and that it was between her and Prescott. That was not the answer I wished for. I wanted to press for more but ultimately held back. Jinx will talk when she wants to.

My mother's actions are unforgivable, and I've been ignoring her calls since. And I'm glad Prescott kicked her out. I would've done much worse, but then again, I'm an asshole. Which makes what I'm about to do so fuckin easier.

Swim practice happens three times a week, and I've been scheming at every one of them for revenge against Liam. That cunt needs to pay for what he did to Ash. And from what I heard, he's planning a party this weekend since Cam can't do it anymore. I think that'll be the perfect time to strike.

"Brother, what's going on in your pea brain?" Ash taps my forehead.

"Liam."

He wiggles his light brows and laughs.

"Fuck off. If I wanted to fuck a dude, I would've done it by now. That cocksucker is going down."

"Yeah, down where?"

"Not on my dick, Ashton. I'm ending him." I bit the words out, knowing full well he's enjoying this conversation.

He shrugs. "That tattoo dick of yours might have enjoyed it. But what's the plan?"

I give him a quick rundown because I usually don't plan anything; plans can change, and I don't like change.

"Jinx cannot go to that party. But I need Maddox to help us."

"She can stay with Spencer. He doesn't seem up for socializing much, anyway. His Batcave is desperate for help."

I slam my locker closed, wrapping my towel around my neck. "Good, now let's scare the shit out of Liam in the water."

"Watch out for Bran. Just because Coach wasn't on our ass doesn't mean this one won't be. I don't like how he stares at you. It's like he wants you."

"Jesus, Ash. You need your dick sucked or fucked."

He stops dead in his tracks. "About that. Jinx did suck my dick," he says softly.

I smiled, knowing how hard it's been on him. I'll never forget that night, either. I thought I knew what hell was, but I wasn't prepared for the nights and weeks following. Picking my brother off the bathroom floor half-dead was never on my list in life. And I never want to do that again.

I reach out, pulling him in for a tight embrace. "I'm proud of you, brother." Pulling away, I cup his face. "Take things at your pace, though, and don't force it if you aren't ready."

He places his hand over mine. "I know, and Jinx knows that."

With a final nod, we both leave the change room. Stepping inside the natatorium, the chlorine smell slams into my nose, reminding me how I ended up here every time. I would quit in a heartbeat, but Ash needs me. The new coach, Bran, glares at us as we sit. He can kiss my ass if he thinks I'm coming out here early.

I scan the stands and spot Jinx instantly. Her raven hair hangs loosely curled to the side, exposing her neck, and just thinking about marking it up makes me not want to be wearing this Speedo. Maddox leans over and whispers something in her ear, and her eyes shift to mine.

Later, she mouths.

Yeah, later, for sure.

Bran blows his whistle and officially cockblocks me.

"Listen up. I'm sure you heard about your captain being suspended, and in the meantime, I will not be replacing him."

"What the hell, Coach? We need a captain!" Emery calls out.

"Why? Hoping it was gonna go to you?" Ash mocks him.

Bran smacks his clipboard against Emery's head. "That's enough. We don't need a captain in swim practice. Do you need help with swimming laps? Because a captain ain't gonna help with that son." He blows his whistle, signaling he's done with this bullshit talk.

As I approach the diving board, Liam walks next to me.

"So, are you coming to my party this weekend?"

"Why? Is it going to be that lame you need me to be there to spice it up?" I roll my shoulders, loosening them up.

"It's not always about your ego, Atticus."

I step on the diving board, tilting my head in his direction. "It's not my ego you have to worry about, Liam. It's what lies behind that."

I should've tormented him until he couldn't take it anymore—played with his head. That would've been the ultimate way to go. Now I need to be more of a little dramatic bitch about it, not how I like to work. But desperate times call for desperate measures. And this needs to get done pronto.

"Whatever, man." He storms away like a little bitch.

I should just drown him.

This week is dragging, and it doesn't help when every class is giving exams. The amount of stress I'm under will make me explode soon. It doesn't help that Jinx has officially gone silent again. That's how I know she's hiding something. Most likely, it was a text from her stalker. Now I'm gonna have to work it out of her. I'll enjoy it, but she most definitely won't. I meet Ash outside of Psych class, where he's practically mauling Jinx.

"Break it up, kids. No one wants to see that shit."

Ash glares at me, but he'll thank me later, and if his hand had moved her skirt up any higher, I would be beating a shit ton of guys up for looking. Jinx walks away into the class leaving us behind.

"She isn't talking much. She'll change the subject if you ask her anything. Try to figure it out. It's driving me insane." He turned and walked away, leaving me to do what needs to be done.

I move quickly, grabbing her by the arm. "We're sitting in the back row today, little grim. I need to help you escape that shell you're stuck in."

She doesn't say anything as we take our seats. I make her go in first so no one can see what I'm about to do. I lean over, moving her hair away from her neck, stroking a finger along her thumping pulse.

"Jinx, just because you don't talk to me doesn't mean I don't pay attention to you. This has nothing to do with your conversation with your dad."

When she doesn't answer, I slowly slide my hand up her thigh, tugging on the hem of her skirt. "I have ways of making you talk. Keep looking forward and don't make a sound."

I stare forward and slide my hand under her skirt. Feeling the outline of her underwear, I slowly move it to the side. She can be silent, but she can never hide how turned on she is. Her hands grip the small table when I swipe her clit, but she never makes a sound.

"That's my girl." I slide a finger inside her wet entrance. She spreads her thighs wider, flexing her hips. But I'm not playing those games. If she doesn't talk, she doesn't come. With long, slow strokes, I take my time.

"Atticus, please."

"Ah, so she does talk. But I told you to keep quiet, didn't I?" I pull my finger out. "Open, clean it off."

She opens her mouth slightly, and I push my finger in, feeling her wet tongue moving around my finger. The feel of it reminds me of her sucking my dick. I bite back the groan when she sucks hard.

"You're playing a dangerous game, Jinx."

"Maybe that's what I want." A defiant look comes into her eyes.

I grab our bags and drag her out of the row of seats. She tries to jerk her hand from my hold, but there's no way I'm letting her go. Jinx should know by now what she's getting herself into. I don't stop until I get close to the janitor's closet.

"Atticus, we can't do this here."

"The fuck we can't, you wanted this, and I'm doing it now. I'm not waiting." I pull the door open. "Get the fuck in and pull that skirt up."

With slow steps, she moves into the darkened closet, places her hand on the shelf, and the other one moves her skirt up her legs. I move in, closing the door before anyone can see that ass. Groaning, I move closer, pressing my body into hers.

"You best hold on tight because I'm not gonna be nice." I unzip my pants and move her thong to the side. I took a deep breath, burying my face into her neck, and drove into her, sinking deep in one powerful thrust. Her body jerked forward as she screamed my name.

"Fuck, Jinx. I could spend all day between your legs. Squeeze harder for me." I bite her neck, driving deep with quick thrusts. Her small moans egg me on for more. "Give me that orgasm, I want to feel you strangle my dick."

"Atticus." She groans, pressing her ass into me.

I move my hand to her clit, and I can feel my climax coming when she grips me tighter. Her legs tremble as she comes all over my dick and floor. It's too much for me to handle that I finish deep inside of her.

"Jesus, Odette." I press a kiss on her neck before standing and tucking my dick back into my pants.

"Don't call me that name." She stands, fixing her skirt.

"I'll call you whatever name I want. Little grim." I grip her chin, pressing my lips to hers. "Now, let me escort you to music. While you fill me in on that text from *Unknown*."

I open the door, bringing in light. When I look back at Jinx, she's gone pale.

Seventeen

Jinx

Fuck you, Atticus stupid Banks.

He always has to stick his nose into my business when he isn't welcome, and I know for a fact his brother told him to. Ashton is just as bad, but he'll never ask or pry in my business. He isn't the asshole out of the two of them. That is left for Atticus.

I say nothing as he practically drags me to Greywood Hall. The text doesn't need repeating. I can't bring myself to look at it again, and *Unknown* is becoming bolder in his messages; I'm afraid it won't be enough no matter what I do.

The guys are doing their best to protect me, but it's not enough. This asshat seems to find me still, he must be having help. That's the only way he knows my location, but I only talk to the guys and Spencer. And I know they would never tell a soul.

"Jinx? Are you doing alright? You haven't said a word since the closet."

"Yeah. I'm fine."

Atticus growls. "You know what they say about that word?"

I roll my eyes. "That it's used when you're depressed, and you don't want to worry your friends that you're being a Debbie downer. Don't worry, Atticus. I mean, I'm fine, as in. I'm all right."

"God, woman, you are pushing your luck today."

I smile sweetly at him as we reach the hall's main doors. "You love it, or you wouldn't be here still. Thanks for the walk, Ace."

Greywood Hall was once my sanction. Now, it feels like my prison. Lula and Piper do nothing to help being here anymore. I'm not sure why I'm trying to succeed in music, and knowing Maddox wants the chance to win in the orchestra, how am I supposed to take that away from him and not feel guilty?

I'm glad Maddox didn't wait for me at the door like I was a five-year-old. It gets embarrassing when they do it. Everyone stares at me already, but adding a six-foot guy who looks way out of my league adds more attention I don't want.

The weird goth girl must be good with her mouth. She must be having sex with all three to keep them around. I can't believe they want to be with her out of all the girls in this school. I wonder if she pays them to hang around her; that's the only way I would be around her.

I've heard all the whispers going through the halls; I'm not invisible to their words, but I'm used to them. This school isn't filled with weirdness like me. It's all preppy uptight; I get all my money from my daddy-type kids. Therefore, I'll treat whoever I want the way I want. If they only knew what I could do to them.

"Baby, ready for this?" Maddox asks, holding out his right hand for me.

"Right, the concert is next week, and we need to play for all the puppets, don't we?"

"Be nice," he said with a slight laugh.

"I am being nice. I could've said worse, and you know it." I'm worried that Lula will get the spotlight without working for it. Unless Von has officially moved on from her, but I highly doubt it. Piper and Lula, at the same time, are a win in his book.

I do my best to ignore everyone when we enter the room and head straight to my cello. I need to play more; I'm sure most of my stress would disappear if I did. Maddox grabs his guitar and tunes it. The melody he is strumming is heaven to my ears. I'll never get tired of hearing my favorite sound in the world.

"Listen up," Von calls out. "I'll call each pair up one by one to take the stage. This is the only chance we all get to watch each other. The concert is next week, please be prepared. This counts toward the orchestra."

Of course, the first person called up is Lula. This is going to be torture.

As much as I love music, I'm damn near falling asleep halfway through the class. I thought having pairs would be quicker. I was sadly mistaken, and Von must be taking his anger out on me or something because there are only five pairs left, and I'm not the only one who looks bored to death. That makes me feel really excited to play.

"Jinx, stop it. Everyone will still love hearing you play." Maddox draws me closer to his body.

"You don't know that. This is your first time playing for all these dickhats. They don't care either way."

"It doesn't matter. All that matters is we get up there and play our best. Then shine even brighter during the concert. We are a team. What you feel, I feel, and I can feel your anxiety eating away at you. Tell me what's going on."

I hate when he can read me like a book. It's unfair, but I can't tell him I feel guilty about all of this. His dream is my dream, and we both can't have it; one of us is going to be broken in the end. Because hells if I'm letting bitch face win.

"I'm just nervous, that's all. I don't like being last." I shrug against his body.

"If that's what you need to tell yourself, I'll go along with it."

By the time we're called up, only three pairs are left. To say that I'm pissed would be an understatement. I try to calm down, but it's no use. Von is moving higher and higher on my shit list. I don't care what Dad says, he needs to hire a new music professor, this is bullshit. It's one thing to treat students like this, but to be having sex with them is way off the chart.

I take my seat and position my cello between my legs, and my body forms around the instrument. I glance at Maddox; he looks relaxed on the stool with his feet planted wide. I start the song off, and he jumps in. The music takes me, and I forget where I am. Nothing matters. My troubles seem like such worthless things to worry about. Being in this school is pointless when I'm playing; nothing can touch me. But even I know that when I'm done, the world will crash down on me and turn everything into darkness again. *Unknown* will be waiting for me around every corner. Maddox's troubles will still be there; nothing I say will help him. He'll never believe me, and he needs to heal from the inside first.

RWA is not for the weak, and I'm afraid for him.

I figured Atticus wouldn't let me get away without telling him about the text message. After classes, he's waiting for me in my dorm room, relaxing on the couch with Edgar on his chest. It's a strange duo if you ask me. But I'm glad they get along. I'm sure he'll be heartbroken when I set him free next week. Edgar is milking his recovery for everything he's got just for those treats—spoiled little shit.

"Atticus, Edgar. Enjoying yourselves?" I place my bag on the table, folding my arms across my chest. "You realize he's a bird, not a dog, correct?"

Atticus covers Edgar's head. "Shh, he has feelings, Jinx." He strokes his chin. "She doesn't mean it, man. She's having a hard day, that's all."

"I can't with you two. Where's your brother?" I ask, moving into the kitchen and grabbing a snack and a treat for Edgar.

"Finding his geek friend."

Geek friend? "What for?"

"Geeks are good for one thing, getting your schoolwork done."

Oh, for fuck's sake. "Why didn't he say he needed help? Either I or Spence could've tutored him."

Atticus laughs. "That takes work, and Ash is lazy. This is easier."

Whatever, I guess.

"Spill it, Jinx. I'm not here to entertain the bird. Tell me or show me the phone."

So much for him forgetting all about it. I walk back to the table, grabbing my bag in anger. All I want is to move past this, but that will never work for me. Digging around until I find my phone, I take a deep breath before opening the text.

Unknown: Odette, I can't get over that dinner. Wow, right.

"You got this when?" Atticus stands, taking my phone from me.

"The day after that so-called family dinner. How would he know about that?"

Atticus glanced behind him, our eyes tangled together. "Jinx, if he knew you were there, that means he was in that house or was watching from outside."

Shivers raced down my back, shaking my entire body. He's been watching my every move; for all I know, he could've been inside the house sitting across from me the whole time. But none of them looked familiar except—Roan.

I tumble on the couch, trying to catch my breath. Can it be Roan? I've never noticed him before. There's no way it can be him. What would he gain from tormenting me like this? Something isn't adding up.

"Jinx, what is it?"

I blink out of my thoughts, shaking my head. "No, well. Maybe it's something. But what if it's Roan?"

"Roan? The douche that was sitting next to you?" He clenched his fists tight, watching me.

"I don't know, it doesn't make sense. Why would Roan stalk me? And why now? I've been here for years."

Atticus kneels in front of me, taking my hands. "Listen to me. When you left the dining room Saturday, your dad blew up on Mother. Roan acted like a knight in shining armor."

My hands tighten around his. "What? Why?" I'm so confused. Dad never mentioned any of this. He only told me that Serena was moving out because things escalated after I left. AKA, I can't keep my mouth shut and pushed them for a divorce.

"I'm certain Roan and Mother know each other. That's why he was there that night, and your dad didn't look like he was buddies with him."

"What do we do now?"

"We act like nothing has changed. If he suspects any-thing, he might escalate, and you would be at risk. I say we always keep our eyes open for Roan. If he comes near you and we aren't around, call. He won't be able to take a shit without one of us around."

I think it's easier for him. He doesn't have to deal with this. What if I don't see him coming until the last second?

These messages won't end either; nothing will end until Roan ends.

Eighteen

Ashton

I can't believe Ace suckered me into this stupid party. I much rather be cuddling on a couch with a pretty
dark-haired woman than trying to weave in and out of
sweaty ass bodies. This music is horrible, the booze is
warm, and Liam has no idea how to throw a party. No
wonder why Cam never let him help plan any.

Why you have to get shitfaced to show off is something
I never understood. Have a few drinks and be a decent
person. I guess getting drugged and raped has jaded me
about college parties. I know Ace understands why I don't
like being here, and I get it's important, but pushing the
memories back is getting complicated.

Maddox wraps his arm around my shoulder, dropping his head to mine. "I got you, brother. Our demons won't win today."

Today, being a keyword. "Thanks. I just want to end this already."

"I know. Give Atticus a little while. We can't jump in feet first. I haven't even seen Liam yet."

Now that he mentions it, I haven't either. He planned this stupid thing, and Liam can't even mingle with his loser friends. Shane and Emery are hanging around the island drinking and trying to pick up some chick with big boobs. What Ace has planned won't work if Liam isn't around.

"Are you sure Jinx is safe tonight?" My stomach crashes just thinking about her. What if that stalker of hers finds her? Now that we suspect it's Roan, anything can happen.

Maddox swallows his beer, and without looking back at me, he says, "Spencer wouldn't let anything happen to her. He knows what would happen to him if he did."

But it's like the Devil has different plans for us because time stands still when the front door opens, and Jinx walks in. She drags Spence onto the makeshift dance floor and dances like no one is watching. Her black jumpsuit shows off every curve when she swings her hips to the music, and a relaxed look washes over her face as she dances.

"She looks calm tonight," Maddox says.

"I was just thinking that it probably has something to do with Cam not being here. I don't want to interrupt her, but Atticus is gonna be pissed."

I can watch her dance for hours, even with her dancing with another man; it's the hottest thing I've seen. Watching her with Mad or Ace fascinates me, but I didn't think this would. Fuck. I adjust my pants before moving toward her. It's my turn.

I move behind her, lightly tracing her spine before grabbing her hips and pressing her ass into my hips. I notice Spence grin at me before he walks off.

"Little swan, what am I going to do with you?" I move a hand around her stomach as we move together.

She angles her head and smirks. "I can think of something, only if you are up for it." She grinds low, pressing on my dick.

I take a deep inhale, filling my lungs with smoke from the surrounding joints and cigarettes. I don't think I'm ready to take this where Jinx wants. Who knows if I'll ever be ready for sex again. I spin her around and pick her up. Her legs wrap around my waist, rocking her hips. I watch as her nipples harden under the dark fabric of her jumpsuit, teasing me with desire.

"Use me, Jinx," I whisper next to her ear. "Show all these people what they can't have."

Doing as she's told, she moves with the beat of the music, her nails dig into my neck when she brings her face closer. "Ash, I'm coming. Oh, God."

I press our lips together, swallowing her moan as she comes on the dance floor. That might have been the hottest thing I've ever seen. I grin against her lips.

"We're gonna get our asses chewed out in ten seconds." I spot Atticus storming in our direction.

"Worth it." She chuckles, resting her head on my shoulder.

"The fuck was that? You realize you are in public. Jesus Christ, Ashton, you should know better," he hissed harshly before looking at Jinx. "Don't even get me started with you. Where the fuck is Spencer?"

Jinx pops her head up, narrowing her eyes. "Leave him alone, this was my idea. It's the only time I can enjoy myself. Don't be a fun sucker, I'm safe here."

He points his finger but doesn't say anything because she's right. Where all here, and if that dickbag stalker of hers does show up, it would look weird. Adults aren't welcome here, and it would be game over instantly.

"Fine, but you stay with Spence. We have shit to do. I mean it, Odette."

She wiggles out of my hold, getting into Atticus's space.

"Listen here." She pokes him in the stomach. "You aren't the boss of me so stop acting like it." She whirled around toward the kitchen without looking back.

"I suggest we work fast before she gets drunk. Where is Liam?"

Ace shakes his head, walking away. I follow where Maddox is still hanging out. Ace nods for him to follow. I hate when he doesn't tell me shit. Why be so secretive? All I asked was a simple question. He leads us down the hallway, past the bathroom, and into the office.

I stop short when I see Liam gagged and tied to a chair in the middle of the room. Blood running down his forehead, past his swollen eye, and onto his white polo top. I turned a questionable gaze to Atticus because this was not part of the plan.

"I went off script," he says with a shrug.

"I'd fuckin' say. What the hell happened!" I point at the douche in the chair. "This isn't going off script, Ace. This is beyond that."

"Either way, I found him, and we have him. Now, can we start already?"

Maddox walks to the desk, opening the top drawer. When he walks back toward us, he's holding a pair of scissors. I watch Liam wiggle his wrists the closer Mad gets. Even if he tried to scream, the music was blaring throughout the house, and no one would hear him.

"This would have been easier if we had the proper tools, but we use what we have. It'll hurt you more than us. But you won't say a word, anyway. You're a fuckin' coward, aren't you, Liam? That's why you always did what

Cameron told you to do." I take the scissors from Maddox. "Next time someone tells you to drown a person, get it done the first time, or don't try at all."

Atticus pries at Liam's hand as I open and close the pair of scissors and smile.

"Which finger are we gonna try to cut off?" Maddox asks.

Liam screams in the cloth that's rammed in his mouth.

"The pinky? Good choice. You'll still be able to swim. Lucky you." He'll be fine, just like I could swim with my head injury. Ace holds his finger, and I position the scissors on the middle joint.

Liam shakes and starts crying. It's sad, really. But he asked for this. I slam the scissors closed, and he screams. This would've been easier with pliers. I open the scissors and repeat the process. The top half of his pinky lays in the puddle of blood on the floor, and Liam has gone still.

"Leave him. Someone will find him." Atticus spits on him before walking away.

I know he wanted to torment Liam and Cameron more, and I know he will if they try anything again. Ace isn't afraid of killing someone; he damn near killed the assholes that sliced Maddox's face.

I take one last glance at Liam before closing the office door behind me. When he wakes up, I hope he thinks about not being friends with those who will never have your back. A true friend will be there when you call in the middle of the night with a stupid plan and ask when and where. They will never try to talk you out of something, and they will have a backup plan, be your ride or die. Those are true friends. Not ones that make you do something stupid and then leave you to the wolves.

Having Atticus by my side is a given; we're stuck with each other for life. Not because we are twins but because we've gone through so much together, nothing separate. It's crazy the more I think about it. It's always as a pair. Even when that bitch raped me, Atticus helped me. He was by my side, feeling my pain like it was his own. I owe him so much for that.

"What in the fuck?" Maddox yells.

My attention swings to where he's looking, and I have the same question. We weren't gone that long, were we?

The dance floor has become a Beer Pong tournament with Spencer and Jinx on one side, booing away as one of the guys across from them throws the ping-pong ball across the table. I've never seen her act like this before. Who the fuck is this Jinx?

"I have so many questions. Where do I begin?" I stare away.

"I know where to begin. It's with that so-called best friend she has." Atticus pushes his way through the crowd.

"Shit, he's gonna cause a scene, isn't he?" Maddox looks at me.

I roll my eyes. "What do you think?"

I don't know what he's going to do. He's been unpredictable lately, and I don't like it. I understand trying to protect Jinx, but he's going to the extreme now that the suspect of her stalker is walking around. If we're around her, she's safe. Playing a little game of Beer Pong isn't going to hurt her.

"Atticus!" I yell. But he ignores me. There is only one way to stop him, which goes against the brotherly code. I walk faster, getting behind him and wrapping my arm around his neck tight.

"The fuck, man."

"I can't let you, and she needs this. Stop acting like an asshole." I tighten my grip, moving his head into my armpit.

"She should be having fun with us, not him." He squirms under my hold.

"Don't try to control her either. Now tell her we're heading back, you say goodbye and we'll wait for her when she returns. Trust me, brother." I wait for him to nod, and then I release him.

She's safe, she isn't alone. If anything were to happen, we would find out.

Nineteen

Jinx

My head hurts, scratch that everything hurts. Last night was a blur after the guys left. They might have given me a little too much freedom. Spencer and I never had that much at a party, and it's because Cam wasn't there, hiding around every corner. I felt safe for once. If only that had stopped me from taking so many shots.

I pull my blanket closer to my chin and roll onto my side, the world can wait another day. It doesn't need me today.

"Wakey wakey eggs and bakey, baby."

"Go away, Maddox. I'm not in the mood for your happiness this morning."

I get pulled across the bed and land next to a warm body. I inhale deeply. The scent of sandalwood calms my woozy stomach. I roll over and bury my nose into Maddox's chest.

"You have to get up," his long fingers worked through my hair. "The twins are fighting again, and I can't get them to stop. I need you to yell at them." He continued to play with my hair, and my body relaxed, becoming heavy on his chest.

"I'm sure they'll get over whatever they are fighting over," I told him, feeling myself zone out. I was almost asleep when a loud crash came from the living room, jolting us both up.

"I warned you. Something is going on with those two."

Maddox helps me out of bed, even though every move makes me want to throw up. I eventually find a pair of joggers and a hoodie hanging on the back of the door. With Maddox leading the way, we enter the living room to find my coffee table broken and Ashton lying on the ground with a bloody nose.

"For the love of Lucy, what the hell, you guys." I try to locate Edgar, but he isn't anywhere to be seen. My heart races when I start thinking the worst, what if one of them landed on him?

"Where is Edgar?" I called out. I dash over to where Edgar usually sleeps; his box is empty. I throw his blanket around, everything else on the counter, and anything else in my way. He isn't here. "Where the hell is he?" My lips trembled around the words.

With a growing sense of doom, the longer I look for him, the more afraid I am that his time has finally come to an end.

"Odette, hey, it's okay," Atticus spoke softly, tilting my chin, his eyes bore into mine. "The window was left open all night, little grim. It's safe to say he flew away because it was his time."

I snapped my eyes to the window. Did I leave it open? I should've known Edgar was ready to leave; his leg had been healed for a while, and I just didn't want to let him go. I enjoyed his company too much. I knew better, though.

"He'll be back. Edgar wouldn't leave you alone, Jinx," Ashton reassures me.

He's right. Edgar always came for a visit every day. I just wanted to be there when he left—I feel so abandoned.

I look over at Ashton, taking in his swollen blood, crusted nose. I had forgotten entirely about what was going on. My poor living room stands destroyed. What could've brought a fight on?

"Explain all this now."

Atticus backs away, looking anywhere but in my direction. That's how I know this fight is about me. And if I have to guess, it's about me staying out with Spencer. I'm not giving up hanging out with my best friend.

"He's mad, Jinx, that's all. I can handle a bloody nose. Sorry about your table. I'll get you a new one. In the meantime, I'm gonna stay in our dorm."

"That doesn't explain anything, Ash. What was the fight about?"

Ashton walks to the kitchen sink, grabs a dishcloth, and turns on the water. He daps the blood from his top lip and leans against the counter facing me.

"Jinx, it's because you don't listen when we tell you to do something, and then this white knight here steps in and lets you get away with anything. The way you two acted last night, don't get me started. Then to let you stay behind with Spencer, and he drops you off fuckin' whacked out of your goddamn mind. I wanted to kill the prick." Atticus paces the living room, not once looking at me.

I look to where Maddox is standing, and he shrugs. Did I piss him off, too? All I wanted was some fun. Since we know who my stalker is, I didn't think anything of it.

"So I'm not allowed any freedom to have fun. Is that what you're telling me?"

"Yes."

"No."

"Maybe."

They all answer.

"I need you all to leave, please. Now," I said emotionlessly. My temples throb with anger the more I think about their answers. Of course, Atticus doesn't think I need freedom. If he had it his way, I would be locked away in my tower.

Maddox takes a step forward but stops. "Jinx, can we explain our answers?"

I shake my head no. "I don't want to hear anything. Just go." I turn, picking up all of Edgar's things. Why, of all days, did he have to fly away?

"I would never hold you back, Jinx. Swans aren't meant to be caged; don't keep us away for too long."

Leave it to Ashton to have the last say. When the door latches closed behind them, I turn around to a broken, quiet dorm. I know I did the right thing because I don't have any regrets; they need to know some boundaries and that they don't run this relationship all the time.

I can't keep going like this.

It's been two days, and they still can't leave me alone. They think I don't see them walking behind me to every class, but it's hard to miss them in a crowd. It also doesn't help when I share classes with them; there is no need to speak with Ashton or Atticus, but it's Maddox that I'm having a hard time with.

The concert is at the end of this week, and neither of us feels confident enough. I don't because of Lula and Piper, and the last time Maddox tried out for a concert, he was attacked. He needs to focus on his music and nothing else.

It's just getting him to believe in himself that I'm struggling with. I can give him all the compliments and encouragement in the world, but it's up to him in the end. I can't control his mindset.

I was halfway to Greywood Hall when I changed my mind. I needed caffeine to deal with all this drama. I spotted Ashton on the steps of the main building, watching me.

Me: Meet me in the food court. I know for a fact you're hungry

Spence is always hungry, and with a chance to ditch class to eat, he'll be here in a matter of seconds. I head for the Raven Bean first. That coffee needs to get into my system more than food. There's just something about this café that speaks to my dark little heart. All the walls are painted black, with strange and unusual oddities hanging in every which way. The jackalope skeleton head is my favorite.

With my coffee and a sandwich for Spence, I find a table in the middle of the food court. I take my psych homework out and try to concentrate, but learning about mental behaviors isn't on my mind at the moment. The sound of books slamming on the table jolts me upright.

A pair of green eyes stare back at me. He drew his eyebrows together in a frown as I searched him over. His cheeks grow pink the longer I look.

"Odette?"

"Who's asking?" I felt my heart flip; no one ever asked for me.

He shoves the books in my direction. "Give those to Ashton and tell him I want my payment." His eyes focused intently on my face.

"Okay? Why can't you give them to him?"

"Can you do it or not?"

"Yeah, it's not a problem."

I watch as he walks away, leaving me with so many questions. I wouldn't call him a geek for being intelligent, but I love the suspenders he wears.

"Teeny, what's the matter?" Spence sits down, adjusting his glasses.

"Nothing, just someone dropping stuff off for Ashton. Here, food for you."

He blows a kiss at me before digging in. I'll never get over how one guy can love food this much; it's a ham sandwich for fuck's sake. He shakes his head and grunts.

"No, Jinx. Something is wrong, spill it."

I lean back in my chair, staring at the ceiling. "Spence, there is so much shit, I don't even know where to start."

"From the beginning. I'm not leaving until you spill everything from that small-breasted chest."

Leave it to him to make fun of my non-existing tits. Amusement glinted in his gray eyes. Even when I want to close up, he has a way of making me smile.

"Edgar flew away two days ago and hasn't been back. Do you think he left me for good?"

He stops chewing, lowering his sandwich, and his face turns serious. "That bird has been with you since he was a baby. Do you honestly think he would leave you?"

I shrug.

"Teeny, Edgar loves you. He's probably off getting his little bird dick wet. He's been in your room for weeks now."

My lip curls. "Jesus, Spence. Don't talk like that."

"What else is eating away at you?"

"Dad and Serena are getting a divorce. I might have escalated things over family dinner, as always. Dad told me she mentioned something about Mom, which was his last straw. I ruined everything, Spencer. Then I kicked the guys out of my life, or at least tried, but they didn't listen. I need some space from their overbearingness."

He nodded his head solemnly. "First, you didn't make your dad do anything. Serena is a giant cunt, and she had this coming. I'm surprised it took your dad this long. Good on him. I don't wanna see her around this school anymore." He smirks. "As for those shining twins, good luck with that. They've been hanging in the back of the café this entire time, watching us. They do have boundary issues. But have you ever thought of why they do it?"

"No." I scoff.

"It's because they love you but won't say it."

"No, they aren't." I burst into laughter.

Spence fixed me with a doubtful look like he knew I knew.

They can't love me. I have too much going on for all that. My phone buzzes on the table, and I'm betting it's one of the guys.

When I turn it over and read it, my body turns to ice.

Unknown: It's been forever since I sent you a message. How many days has it been? Doesn't matter now, does it? I saw you at the house party. I wish it were me you were getting off on, just thinking about it makes my cock hard. One day.

Twenty

Maddox

I'm drowning again. Without Jinx around, I'm not gonna make it through the darkness. I knew she would lie and leave me again. This is why I don't trust people. I rev my car, pushing it to go faster. I need to get away. I don't care where I end up, anywhere, but RWA is better.

I know I shouldn't be taking it out on her, but I can't help it. She's been ignoring me for days, even with the huge concert coming up, and it's my one and only chance to prove myself. She can't even show up to practice for me. I was left alone in the hall while everyone else was having a great time with their partner, and I was left dying inside. Ace told me she had coffee with Spence instead of showing up for me. I'm replaceable.

I'm not even sure why I'm still here. Everyone is better off without me. It's why my parents left. They knew back then I was a shit person and would drag them down.

My phone rings for the third time, but I ignore it. I don't care who it is, and they only call when they need something. It's funny how that works, but when I need them, where are they? Too busy following Jinx around.

I pull into the parking lot of the nearest liquor store. It's time to buy my best friend, Jack. He never does me wrong. The cashier side-eyes me the entire time I'm in the store. Don't blame him; if he knew what I was planning, I would be watching me, too.

"Rough day?" He asks, bagging my bottle.

"Something like that." I hand him a twenty.

He hands me the bag, and he doesn't let go when I reach for it. "Remember, kid, the sun still shines even on your darkest days. You just have to figure out who that sun is."

Jinx flashes in my mind; she is my sun. But right now, it's too dark to see any brightness.

"Thanks." I rip the bag from his hand and head out. After this bottle, the only thing I'll see is the inside of a toilet or maybe a fuckin ditch if I'm lucky enough. I'm hoping for something permanent. I don't even wait to get in the car before cracking the bottle open.

I welcome the burn of the first taste. The last is my favorite, by then, I can't remember why I started drinking, but by then, it doesn't matter. The mind is a clouded mess, and that's the end goal. My phone rings again, and you would think they would get the message. Without looking at it, I toss it into the glove box.

The sun is setting, and I'm still breathing.

I roll the window down and throw the empty bottle out. That idea didn't work. All my pills are in my dorm. If I want those, I'll have to sneak back in. The odds that one of the twins isn't in my room will be slim. It'll be worth it. At this point, I don't even care.

Why can't I just succeed at one thing in my life? My phone stopped ringing hours ago, they gave up on me again. I'm not even good enough to keep trying to get a hold of. The school comes into view, and my heart sinks. I don't want to be here anymore. I should've stayed in Grovedale; that's where trash belongs. I park the car, and I'm surprised I don't have any babysitters waiting for me. I take the first step out, and the world tilts.

Maybe Jacky Boy did do his job after all.

Catching myself with the door, I chuckle to myself. It's a long walk to Darrow Hall if I even make it. And these woods give me the creeps, I swear something, or someone, is watching me. Maybe it's a wolf, and they can eat me. I'll be their Little Red Riding Hood. Fuck I must be wasted if I wanna turn into little red.

I need those pills and more booze. The closer I get to the dorms, the louder it becomes. Can't anyone stay in, this school doesn't have a fascinating nightlife. By the time I reach the back doors, I contemplate passing out on the steps. Walking up four flights seems like a lot of energy. Maybe I'll slip and break my neck.

With a groan, I slowly make my way to my room. I'm surprised my phone hasn't rung again. Speaking of my phone. I pat down my pockets but don't feel it, guess I left it in the car. Oh well. My head spins the more steps I take, and I can't even remember what floor I'm on.

"Maddox? What the fuck. We've been looking for you for hours," Ashton demeaned, staring at me from the top of the stairs.

I wave him off and stumble. "Leave me alone." I push past him, but his hand clamps down on my shoulder.

"Talk to me, goose. What's going on?"

"She fuckin' left me, Ashton. She straight up lied to me. How can I ever trust her again?" I take a deep breath, trying not to lose it on him. It's not his fault.

"Let me help you. I'm surprised you made it up those stairs. What the hell were you thinking?"

I spread my arms wide. "I was thinking about killing myself, but here we are." I brush him off and keep walking.

"Maddox!" he yells.

I flip him the middle finger. He'll follow me, anyway. Now that he knows what I tried doing, he won't leave me alone. It's how our relationship goes; I'm selfish, and he picks up after me. I hope one day he learns just to leave me alone.

"Maddox, wait. Don't go in there."

I opened my door and immediately regretted it. I'm not drunk enough for this.

"Don't even think about leaving, Maddox Van Doren. Get your drunk ass inside now." You couldn't miss the disappointment in Atticus's voice.

"What, Atticus? I have nothing to say. Let me pass out before you start lecturing me." I grit my teeth, and my head is beginning to pound. I can't deal with this shit.

I make it to my room, flick on the light, and curled up in my bed is Jinx. If this was supposed to be an intervention, it sucks. I kick my shoes off, not giving a shit where they land. When I get near the bed, I tug my T-shirt off and toss it behind me. I pull the covers away slowly and slip in next to Jinx. She rolls over and wraps her arm around my stomach, sliding closer to me.

"I missed you today. Sorry about ditching you. I needed to talk to Spence. Forgive me?" her voice drifted back to sleep.

As usual, I flew off the handle. I'm sure half the phone calls were from Jinx. The last thing I remember is the lights going dark and my mind going blank. Sleep found me before my demons did.

A light sensation down my chest causes me to stir awake. Without thinking, I pull Jinx flush against my chest. Her soft curves melt against me, and I breathe in her coconut scent. Having her here calms me, making yesterday seem like years ago. And making me realize I was a giant fuckin' douche.

Her fingers slowly weave into my hair. "Don't you ever feel like you have to run away from me again. Just because I needed space doesn't mean I wanted to leave you. Having three guys around all the time is suffocating. But if anything happened to you, Maddox," her words trail off, a tear lands on my bare chest.

I pull her closer. "I'm sorry, baby. I wasn't thinking, that's my problem. I never do."

"I should've worded it better. It's on me." She buries her face into my neck. "I'm sorry."

"I can't let you take the blame for my problems, Jinx. It's not your burden; I need to work on myself."

She sits halfway up, watching me. "But I'm here, and you don't need to do anything alone. Ashton and Atticus are here as well. Stop doing things alone."

I'll always be alone, even with them around. They don't understand that. I don't like to depend on others for help. Eventually, they'll leave me.

Her finger taps my forehead. "Get out of there. Those voices are harmful, and we don't listen to negative thoughts around here. Now we have a concert in two days, can we still practice together?"

"Seriously?" I shift into a seating position, taking her with me until she's straddling me. She traces random shapes on my skin, sending shivers down my body.

"My cello is in the living room, wanna show the guys what we've been working on?"

I never thought about getting in front of a crowd, let alone a large crowd, until now. What if I royally fuck up? Not only would I be ruining my future, but Jinx's as well. I can't do that to her. I was selfish for asking her to be my partner. All I saw was the end goal, getting out and never returning.

"Come on, we'll head down to Greywood and practice there. It's just what the doctor ordered."

She hops off, grabbing her pants. She opened my closet and dug through my hoodies until she found a black one.

"You know there are different colors in the world. Have you tried them yet?"

She chuckles, pulling the hoodie over her head. "I have when I was a child. Then I grew up and realized the world is a dark place." Her look turns serious.

I might have known her for years, but maybe I don't know her. I only ever hung out with the twins when she lived at home; it wasn't until I moved here that I started to talk more with her. I've never seen her wear anything but black. A person can't go through life wearing one shade.

"Are you okay, Jinx?"

"I'm good, just a lot on my mind. Once this concert is over and Von dick hole tells us who he picks, things will be less stressful for me. I'm sure he'll pick Lula, though."

I move toward her, cupping her face. "Von would be stupid not to pick you. You are talented."

"He should pick you if he is smart." She shrugs.

"Let's just get through this first and then see what happens. I'm not feeling very optimistic about the future at the moment. I'll play my best, but that's all I'm willing to do."

I move a hand around her hand, pulling her into my chest. Her small hands wrap around my waist, squeezing me tight. "I'll play my best, too, baby."

"Good, just don't get angry and throw a punch when he doesn't pick you. I'll do that. I can't get kicked out of this school."

"The perks of owning it," I said with a laugh.

"You know it, big guy."

Twenty-One

Atticus

To say that I'm pissed at this entire situation wouldn't be enough. Jinx is still getting messages from her little stalker. I refuse to call him by his name. To know he was watching her at the party doesn't sit well with me. How did I not notice him? Liam is being a little bitch about his finger. The entire time at swim practice, he kept complaining to Bran and wouldn't get in the water. Luckily, he wouldn't say a word about how he lost most of his pinky. If Liam did, I would take another one.

Now I have no choice but to attend a concert. Mother made a big deal about attending as a family, but I'm unsure why. She hates Jinx and never wanted to do anything for her before. After Prescott kicked her out, it's like she's trying to make things right. I'm sure that ship has sailed. He doesn't want her back, and I don't blame him.

I've never stepped foot in Greywood Hall before. Being a band geek wasn't my thing, but this hall is massive. I figured it was one room, but they have multiple rooms for practices and classes. I follow Ash and the crowd to the concert hall. This school didn't waste a dime on interior decorations, that's for sure.

Three rows of red seats flood the first floor to the stage. Looking around, I notice the walls are lined with black panels leading to a curved cathedral ceiling. If a vampire jumps out, I wouldn't be surprised. When I look at the stage, I notice a black, glossy grand piano sitting in the middle with a spotlight shining on it. I'll admit it would be amazing to know how to play one, but I wouldn't have the patience to learn anything but the chopsticks.

"This place is interesting," Ash whispers as we take our seats.

I nod, agreeing, taking in the small raven carvings along the stage. "Yeah, you could say that again."

"I thought Prescott would've been here before us." Ash swings around, looking at the doors.

It is a little strange. "Maybe he's in the back with Jinx."

"That would make sense. He is the Dean, after all. But where is Mom?"

I take in the room. She should've been here by now, too.

"I swear if they are in the bathroom having sex, I'm gonna barf." Ash covers his mouth.

"I highly doubt that. Prescott looked serious when he kicked her out. I don't think he's getting his rocks off in the bathroom in a music hall."

"True. She's probably giving Roan a blowjob."

Fuckin' Roan.

The lights dim, and the curtains close. "Maybe we should've texted them."

Ash shrugs. "Sucks to be them. Good parents would've been here before the kids."

That's the thing. Prescott is a good parent unless he's staying with Jinx until she goes on. This is a big thing for her. Von is a dickhead for not choosing her. He shouldn't be allowed to teach here; sleeping with your students is disgusting. Then again, I'm sleeping with my step-sister, but it's worth it. And I guess if Prescott divorces my mother, Jinx won't be my stepsister; she'll just be Jinx.

The first pair takes the stage, and it's a violin and some other loud and annoying instrument you blow into. I don't think my ears are going to last until Maddox and Jinx take the stage. I need a fuckin' joint.

"I'll be back. I need a quick breather."

"Be quick. I don't know when they're coming on."

I duck between each person in our row, getting a few angry looks. I glare back at the old lady in the last seat when she doesn't move.

"A heart attack is in your future. I'll manifest it for you."

Her eyes widen with shock as I leave. I don't have time for petty people, and this school is filled with them. I know I'm an asshole, but only to those that deserve it, and that's mostly every person I encounter.

This place makes me insane; stepping outside in the cool air feels perfect. I dig the joint out of my pocket and light it. This will make the evening more tolerable, or even this text I have to send.

Me: Where are you? You wanted this to be a stupid family event and can't even show up. Typical.

What I really wanted to say to her was quit sucking Roan's dick and get over here. But that would be pointless. I take one more puff and put my joint out. Ash would be pissed if I missed Jinx on stage. I would be, too, and I wanna see Maddox play. It's his second chance up there tonight.

This time, the old lady moved for me, I guess she doesn't wanna die. If only I held that power. Ashton rolls his eyes when I sit.

"God, this sucks. Are my ears bleeding? Give me that joint. Half of these people probably wouldn't mind getting stoned."

I stifled a laugh, and he was probably right. "It can't be that bad." Two chicks are on stage, and one is playing the violin.

"How much longer do you think?" he asked with a curl to his lip.

"I'm not sure. Jinx didn't know either. But I'm hoping it's soon. I sent a message to Mother, but she never did reply."

He shook his head. "Doesn't surprise me, to be honest. She never did care about this shit. Not sure why we should be bothered by it now."

He's right. She's always been a flaky mother. I'm sure that's why our father never came around after a while. He didn't want to deal with her, and Ash and I suffered because of it. I'm sure she doesn't even care that we grew up without a father. Just all her boyfriends coming and going. Prescott has been the longest relationship, and in the beginning, I hated him and figured he would be like every other guy. He's the only one who cares about our future.

The curtains close, letting my ears get some rest.

"They better be next, or I'm headed back outside."

"Fuck you, it's my turn, asshole."

I watch as the red velvet curtains slowly open, and I lose my breath.

My little grim looks like a little vixen sitting on stage. Jinx looks so elegant sitting in a strapless black ball gown.

I'm jealous of her cello sitting between her legs, and when she moves her left leg, it becomes visible from under her dress. One wrong move, and the crowd will see more than they should.

I watch Maddox move his stool beside her and position his guitar on his lap. He looks nervous yet excited to be up there with her. I haven't heard him play much, and never together. The slight tilt of her head and a wink, and I know she's trying to calm him down.

The first swipe of her bow, and I'm already carried away, but when Maddox starts playing. Wow. They make the perfect team. Ashton places his hand on my shoulder, giving it a light squeeze.

"Amazing, aren't they, brother?" he asks, memorized by them.

I can't take my eyes off them either. "They are. I'm proud of Maddox."

"He deserves it, but what if he doesn't get picked? What if Jinx gets picked? What do you think will happen?"

I watch Jinx sway along to the music, knowing deep down what she would do if she were picked. She would sacrifice her winning for Maddox to get him out of this place. That's the thing about Jinx; she always places everyone before herself. It's annoying in some ways. Jinx deserves to get out, too; it has been her dream for years. That's all she talked about was getting out of this shitty place.

"The way that Von acts, it's hard to say. I wish Prescott would do something about all the shit professors at this school."

They both stand and take a bow. Ashton and I stand, giving them the loudest applause.

"Let's get backstage and get our girl."

Backstage isn't what I was expecting—as in, there is no backstage. Small dressing rooms line the side of the back of the concert hall, and it's busy with people moving instruments. When we reach the doorway, I spot a cascade of jet-black hair turning into the last room.

Maddox is on his knees, hugging Jinx tight around the waist. Her fingers work through his hair, along his jaw, lightly touching his scar.

"You did it. You showed them how remarkable you are, Maddox, and nobody stopped you. I'm so proud of you."

Her eyes met his, and a smile ran across her lips. He pulls her down fast, making her laugh.

"Thank you, Jinx." His kiss was featherlight. "I owe you so much." Giving her one last kiss, he stands her back up.

"She's right, you know. Fuck what anybody says. You owned that stage tonight," I tell Maddox, walking into the small room.

"Yeah, M. That shit was wicked. Who knew some kid without a dream could pull that off," Ashton said, laughing, pulling Maddox in a tight grip. "I'm so proud of you, brother."

"I can't believe I did that. I thought for sure I was gonna barf."

Jinx shook her head, smiling. "I told you, picture everyone naked."

Fuck, I hope not. Although he'd already seen me naked, half that crowd were old ladies. That wouldn't work so well.

"When do you know if you won or not?" I shake those thoughts out of my head.

Jinx rolls her eyes. "Monday, even though I'm sure I know who won, so it doesn't matter. All that matters is we had a good time."

"The view from where we were was perfection, but if you opened your legs anymore, the row in front of us would've been walking away happy, little swan."

My phone buzzes. It's probably Mother finally getting a hold of us, which reminds me.

"Where's your dad? He never sat with us."

"I don't know. I've been trying to get a hold of him all night. It's not like him to miss a concert." She moves to her bag, digging out her phone.

Witch: I'm sorry about tonight

Me: Are you? You wanted this to happen, and then you ditch out. I'm not surprised.

Witch: I was busy.

I glance at Jinx, and she's shaking.

"What's wrong, Jinx?"

"It's Dad."

Twenty-Two

Jinx

My world is spiraling. Tonight was supposed to be the best night of my life. I should be out celebrating with the guys, cheering Maddox on his huge accomplishment, and mentally killing Von, Lula, and Piper because we all know how that's gonna be going—a nasty threesome.

Instead, I am racing across the courtyard to the main building in a stupid dress I shouldn't be wearing. I knew I should've gone and found Dad before I went on that stage. He has never been late to one of my concerts in all these years. I wasn't thinking straight.

The flashing lights coming down the road made my heart sink to my stomach when Florence sent me a message. She didn't say much, just that Dad was in his office and to come quick. My fear is he had a heart attack earlier, and no one noticed.

I race into the office where Florence waits, silent tears rolling down her cheek. When she sees me, she stands, sending her office chair flying across the small space.

"Odette, I'm sorry. I should've checked on him sooner. I haven't moved him. I was waiting for the paramedics."

"I need to see him." I swallow the lump creeping up my throat. I won't believe anything until I see him.

"Jinx, you don't want to go in there. You have no clue what you'll find." Atticus grabs my wrist. "Seriously, Jinx, don't go in there."

I pull out of his grip. "I need to. You can come, but I'm going."

"Baby, I think you should wait for the paramedics."

"Listen to them, Odette. Stay out of there. Please," Florence begs.

I ignore them, moving down the hallway. The wooden doors I've walked through countless times now seem like a brick wall. Once I cross them, my life will forever be changed. The future will be written in stone, and I won't be able to change it. With a shaky hand, I slowly push the door open.

The office is dark, and a coppery scent fills the air. Why wouldn't Florence tell me about the blood?

"Jinx, don't go any further. I think this is a crime scene," Ashton spoke in a strained voice.

I take another step further, and the outline of Dad collapsed on his desk comes into view.

"Dad?" my voice croaking the closer I got to him. My hand trembled as I reached for him. A hand wraps around my wrist, pulling it away.

"Stop. You don't have to do this alone. We are here with you."

I turn and take in a watery vision of Atticus. "Okay," I mutter.

Ashton moves around, placing a finger on Dad's neck. He turned his face, and his gaze slipped to the floor.

My world ended in that second.

The brain is a funny thing. It has a way of protecting you when it thinks it needs to. I need to remember this moment to recall how Dad looked for the last time. But the only thing I can remember is when he came and visited me in my dorm the other day before the concert, telling me how proud he was and how he couldn't wait to cheer for me. He will forever be my biggest supporter.

Atticus pulls me out of the way as the paramedics rush into the office and move to where Dad is resting. When they pull him away from the desk, my knees buckle when I see the hole in his chest. Atticus wraps his arms around me tighter.

"What the fuck," Maddox whispered, gobsmacked.

"Where the fuck is his heart?" Ashton called out.

Atticus crushes me closer to his chest as I watch in horror; somebody has taken my dad's heart.

"Little grim, let's go. You don't need to watch this." He pulls me from the room, and my brain finally kicks in.

"No, you can't make me leave him." I fight back, digging my heels into the floor.

"I'm not doing this with you." He lifts me over his shoulder.

I punch at his back. "Atticus, stop. I can't leave him. He needs me." I cry out.

It hurts to breathe. Why would anyone want to hurt him? I don't understand any of this. He's always been a caring and understanding man. He would never hurt anyone, so why would anyone hurt him?

"Atticus, why?"

"I don't know, Jinx." He slides me down his body, holding me across his arms. "I'll hold you until I can't anymore. The guys will get some answers." Pressing a kiss to my forehead, he sits in one of the seats by the main office door.

"Oh, Odette. I'm sorry, dear. What can I do?" Florence drops to her knees, brushing my hair away from my eyes.

"What do you know?"

"I don't know much, dear. I left early because everyone was preparing for the concert. I wasn't needed. Your dad was staying behind to finish some paperwork before heading over to the hall. I came back because I forgot my glasses. That's all I know." She rubs her nose and sniffs.

I reach for her hand, giving it a tight squeeze. "It'll be okay, Florence. I won't stop until I find out who did this to him."

"I'm going to go if you need anything at all. Call me." She kissed my forehead and rested a hand on Atticus's shoulder. "Call me if anything happens, sweetheart."

"I will, Florence," he tells her.

Maddox and Ashton appear, looking grim. I sit up, expecting them to tell me anything. But they shake their heads.

"You should look away, baby. The paramedics are bringing your dad out."

As the gurney turns the corner and the black body bag lies on top, I push out of Atticus's arms and fall to the floor. Numbness it's all that's going through my body. I want to wake up from this dream; it must be a dream.

"Are you Odette Hawthorne?"

"Who the fuck would she be?" Ashton exploded.

"Son, you best take it down. We need to talk with her, not you."

"Ash, it's fine." I stand on shaky legs. "I can talk with the officer."

Atticus helps me walk out of the office with the officer and Ashton following behind. The halls of the school I once loved now echo with footsteps of grief.

Ashton stands next to Atticus and me while the officer stares at us. He clears his throat.

"Miss Hawthorne, I need to ask a few questions if that's okay?"

I nod, not trusting my voice.

"Did your dad have any enemies that you know of?"

I drew in a harsh, deep breath. "No. Everyone loved him."

"Officer. Prescott is—was generous," Ashton said with a shake of his head. "You should call his wife if you need these kinds of answers."

"What's her name?"

"Serena," I spit out.

I swear if she had anything to do with this, she better start fuckin' praying.

It's been a week without Dad. Every day, it gets harder and harder to hang on. I made the decision to keep the school open, knowing Dad it's what he would've wanted. I just don't know how I'm going to survive without him. He's been my entire world. And tomorrow, I'll be laying him to rest. It's too much for me to handle. I want to disappear and never return. On top of that, Edgar hasn't been back.

I got Spence to drive me back to the house. I needed space from the guys. The more they crowd around me, the more suffocated I become. Sitting on the back deck reminds me of when I first got my cello. Dad would sit in the chair drinking his coffee as I practiced for him. I was a shitty player, yet he smiled through the entire thing. That's where he sat every afternoon when he got home, and I dragged my cello out here—always supporting my dream of getting into the symphony.

Now, I don't even care. I haven't even bothered to see if Von had chosen anyone. The announcement of a new dean won't be made until next week. The board members want a meeting with the new owner. I'm not ready for that yet. I'm not prepared for any of this.

I just want answers. The cops haven't been much help to find Dad's killer, and Serena keeps nagging me about Dad's will. He was murdered, and she's worried about what she's walking away with. The only nice thing is my stalker hasn't reached out since. I'm hoping that's a good sign.

The back gate opens, and Maddox comes walking through. He's dressed in a black leather jacket and a black beanie. His lazy smile sends butterflies dancing in my stomach. He stops at the bottom step.

He reaches for my hand, and my body tingles from his touch. I wrap my arms around his waist, pressing my face into his chest. A small sob escapes, and I tighten my grip.

"Shh, baby." He pushes his fingers through my hair, rubbing at the base of my nape. "You cry whenever you need to, mourn when you want to. There is no time frame."

I nod against his shirt. I want the pain to go away, to wake up without having a knife in my chest.

"Did you need help to pick out a suit for him?"

"No." I sniff. "I did that already. I was just remembering, that's all."

Maddox tilts my head back, wiping my tears away. "He loved you. Your dad was an amazing guy. I loved him like he was my own." Tears swarm his eyes. "I owe him so much."

"I won't stop until I find out who did this to him."

"We all won't, baby. But I need you to come back with me. Tomorrow is going to be a hard one, and you need to be with people that love you."

That's not what I need. I need names and revenge.

Twenty-Three

Ashton

Let us take a moment of silence, a moment to say our final goodbyes, a moment to find peace. Let us carry Prescott in our hearts as we continue our own journeys.

Those were the last words spoken at Prescott's funeral. Our own journeys. It's a little complicated when Jinx is on her knees, crying her eyes out next to her mother's tombstone and her father's open grave. Her parents are gone, and she has no one.

Then I look over and see Mom. Not a single tear has fallen. I wonder if she even cares that Prescott has been murdered, his heart cut from his chest. And she has the balls to stand there next to fuckin' Roan and not cry. What a witch.

I feel so hopeless; there's nothing to do to take away Jinx's pain. All I can do is watch her cry. I wish there were more I could do for her.

What I want most is to find out who killed her father. The killer has to be in this school. And these cops refuse to do anything. How hard is it to investigate? Not a single suspect, my ass. They just don't want to do their job.

As everyone descends, Jinx stays on the ground.

"What can we do for her?" Maddox asks, never taking his eyes off her.

"There isn't much we can do except be here for her," Atticus answers, looking heartbroken.

We know we've been overcrowding her, but it's what we felt was right. Prescott might have been in our lives for a short while, but we also feel his loss. Who am I going to tease over family dinners now? Who will stick up for me when a professor tries to get me cut from the swim team? In a way, he was like a father to me. He tried to love me, and I didn't want it.

All I have now is her. Why is she still here? I walk away from the guys and storm across the cemetery site. Roan looks up, and his smile fades. Who smiles at a funeral?

"Ashton, so good to see you, son." She fake sniffles.

"Cut the shit, Mom. Why are you here?"

She places a perfectly manicured hand on her chest. "Prescott was my husband."

I turn to Roan. "Then why bring the dick along? Gonna give him a blowjob on top of the fresh grave?"

"Watch your mouth. You don't speak to your mother like that," Roan grits out.

I spit on the ground next to his glossy black shoes. "I don't listen to assholes. Certainly those who sleep with my mom. You know she's only with you for your money. Once she gets what she wants, she's gone."

Mom opens and closes her mouth like a fish out of water. "I do not."

I roll my eyes. "Yeah, and I'm a golden child. Get the fuck out of here."

Jinx's cry of grief grabs my attention. I spin around to see her lying on the ground, shaking. I rush over, dropping to my knees and hauling her into me.

"I've got you. You aren't alone." I try to soothe her.

She wraps her arms around my neck and releases her sorrows. From the corner of my eye, I see Roan watching with something dark in his eyes. He's lucky I never threw him in that fuckin hole and buried him. The nerve to show up here but to keep watching Jinx; it's like he wants to get caught.

"Ash, we should get out of here. It's getting cold, and the last thing we need is for Jinx to catch a cold." Atticus leans down, swiping a piece of hair away from Jinx's forehead.

"Can you take her back? I have something I need to do." I look up at Ace and exchange a silent plea.

He bends down and scoops her up. "Don't take too long. I'll bring her back to our dorm."

I watch Atticus and Maddox leave with her and notice Roan finally walking away. Being back in Grovedale doesn't bring back the best memories. Too many horrible things happen in this town, so it's no wonder Jinx wants to get out so badly. I head out of the cemetery toward the college, where most of the demons lie, not only for me but also for Maddox.

This school wasn't supposed to be where I was meant to go, and I know that now. I should've fought harder at the time and told Prescott no. RWA was where I should've gone from the start. But I wanted Jinx to have her freedom. She needed to get away from us. More so, Atticus.

The more I think about it, the more I wonder if we brought her stalker to her. She never had an issue until we showed up. Maybe it's for the best if we don't return at all. Now that her dad is gone, what will happen? She will have a challenging journey ahead of her now, the owner of an entire school that no one knows about. That's one huge secret to keep.

I need a way for Roan to leave. That'll keep her safe. I hope.

Grovedale College is the simplest college to break into. They never did fix their security for the aqua center. And to blow off steam, I need a good swim. The smell of chlorine is like home to me. Swimming soothes me, and seeing Mom today, I need the water more than anything.

The first dive into the water reminds me why I love this and am so thankful for Prescott. Even if it was Atticus that got us into trouble in the first place, I'm glad swimming was our punishment. Without it, I'm not sure where I would be. I would probably be high as fuck buying random shit still.

It hasn't sunk in that Prescott is gone.

"Boys, Odette will show you around the school tomorrow. It's different from your last one. The rules are stricter. Don't give me a bad name."

Jinx stares at Prescott from across the dining room table. "Dad, we talked about this." She hissed.

"That's enough. They are your brothers. Treat them as such."

Atticus grinned. She may be our stepsister, but he wouldn't treat her as such. Fuck I won't either. The way Ace keeps staring, I won't dare get in the way.

"What's so great about this school?" Ace asks without taking his eyes off Jinx.

Prescott groans. "It will set you up for your future, Atticus. You can't be a lowlife forever. Don't you have plans for the future?"

"Sure. Not to be like my father."

"Yeah, he was a good magician, but it's not for us," I add.

Jinx shakes her head. "That's not what he means. Don't you have ambitions?"

"One," Is all Ace says.

I kick him from under the table. He needs to cool it with the hints, or Prescott will have our heads, and I'm rather fond of both of mine. If he finds out we want to ruin his daughter, we're fucked.

"This school has a wide range of clubs you can join, and I'm sure you'll find something to love. Now, I'll leave you three alone, and it will be you three for a very long time. Don't start shit if you can't finish it."

If he only knew when he said it, it would be accurate, except we have Maddox in our circle now. We have to work together and keep that circle tight.

I make it back to the dorms late. It's later than I expected, and everyone is passed out. I take advantage and head to the laundry room. Digging the joint out of my pocket, I place it between my lips as I walk into the room. I'm about to light it when someone clears their throat.

"Ashton, you aren't supposed to smoke in the building."

I drew in a lungful of air, trying to calm myself. "And geeks are supposed to be in bed by eight."

I watched as his nostrils twitched. "Where's my payment?"

I light my joint, closing my eyes as I inhale deeply. "When I pass my class. I don't trust you, Arch. You fucked me over once already."

"T-that was a mistake. I did the work for you."

His eyes fix upon my lips when I move the joint. "What else do you want?"

He snaps his eyes to the ground. "Nothing."

"Do I not treat you well, Archie?"

His eyes flick up to mine. "You do, I swear."

I move closer, placing the joint between his lips. "Suck."

He draws a deep inhale, coughing immediately. "Oh, dear god. That burns."

"Yeah, the first hit usually does. Just so you know. If you rat me out, I'll rat you out. My little stoner friend."

"What?" he coughs.

"You heard me. Don't be smoking in the laundry room, Archie. It's against the rules. Aren't geeks all for following the rules?" I finish the joint before walking out.

That should teach the prick to fuck with me again. I meant to get back at him for almost getting me kicked off the swim team, and the opportunity fell into my lap. Although I wonder if he could've helped dig some information into Roan for me, that guy popped up like nothing. I don't like it. And to keep texting Jinx like we don't know it's him. What a piece of shit.

I'll do everything I can to keep Jinx safe until we find a way to remove Roan or Jinx from this school.

Twenty-Four

Jinx

Unknown: Odette. My sweet Odette. Our time will come, mark my word.

Unknown: There isn't any point in ignoring me. I see you around campus, and if I wanted to, I could take you away whenever I wanted to. You think those boyfriends of yours would stop me? Think again.

Unknown: Stop the bullshit. Odette. Answer your phone before something happens to you.

The text messages won't stop. I had to turn my phone off. It was getting to be way too much stress for me to handle. It's bad enough that I'm heading into a board member meeting full of douche canoes that hate me.

Let alone know that I'm the new owner of this lovely establishment.

I haven't cried in two days, and that's a win in my books. Dad wouldn't want me going into this meeting looking like a puffy bag of shit. Adjusting my pantsuit, I push open the doors to the boardroom. My heels click along the stone floor.

Barnaby, Archer, and Roan straighten in their seats as I walk further into the room.

Archer rises from his seat as I reach the table. "And what do we owe the pleasure, Odette? We have a meeting with the new owner soon."

I hate that man. I pull out the seat that Dad always occupied, trying to find the strength to continue.

"As most of you know, Prescott passed away, leaving the school to a new owner."

Barnaby hums.

"Yes, we get that. Such shame," Archer retorted testily.

I grit my teeth together, trying to keep my anger at bay. The last thing I need is going off on this old asshole.

"Archer, let the girl speak," Roan tells him.

I'm sure he knows where this is headed since he's already sleeping with Serena.

"Since I'm his daughter, I'm the new owner." I cut to the chase.

Archer slams his hands on the table. "Fuck this shit."

Burnaby leans back in his seat, staying quiet.

And Roan stares at me, his eyes darkening, sending shivers down my spine.

"And as the new owner, Archer. I would be watching that mouth of yours because I can and will kick you off the board. I'm not my father, and I don't care what you say. And your grandson will never step back in this school."

His nostrils flared in anger. "This won't last, Odette. A woman cannot run a school."

I lean further over the table. "Tell that to the person who murdered my father. They should've thought about that in the first place. Sit the fuck down so we can talk about this shit. I have a class to get to."

I'm going to say this is the anger stage of grief because I can't handle this shit today. I should've known this would happen when I walked in here, but this much? Why Dad kept Archer on the board still bothers me. He isn't helpful. All he does is bitch and complain. If it's the money, that's not a good reason to keep someone around. Legacy or not, he's a useless douche.

I swear if Archer steps out of line one more time, he's gone. I don't need him anymore.

Dad's office is the one place I haven't been able to go back into. Considering I need to hire a new dean, I need things inside that office. The caution tape hanging from his doors turns my stomach. His heart is missing, the one thing that held the most love someone stole from him. I buried him without it.

"Odette?"

"Florence, can you go in there for me?" I swing around, coming face to face with Florence.

She shakes her head. "No, dear."

My heart pounds in my throat. I can't go in there; she can't force me.

"Dear, we'll do this together," she said, clutching my arm.

We both inhale and push the door open. The room has a stale smell and nothing like how I used to remember it. Nothing in this office will ever be the same. I hate it already.

"Find what you need, and I'll do the rest. We can't go too long without a dean. Not to rush you or anything."

"No, I know. It's weird, that's all."

"The files you need are in the desk drawer; he never kept anything like that in his computer. He was old school like that."

Swallowing hard, I move around the desk and make the mistake of glancing at the floor. The dark stain glares back at me. Why didn't anyone clean it up? Isn't that a part of their job? Bracing myself on the desk, I slide open the top drawer. A picture of Dad, Mom, and me as a newborn sits in a gold frame. I've never seen this picture before. Why has he never shown this to me? I look like my mom; her dark hair and green eyes are like mine.

"Dear? Are you all right?"

"Yeah," I swallow the lump. "I—Dad never showed me this before." I hold up the frame showing Florence.

She steps forward, gently taking it from me. "A precious moment, frozen in time," she smiled sweetly as she said it.

"What am I gonna do now? I have no one." Pain gripped my chest, taking my breath away.

Florence clutches my shoulder. "You are going to push on, be the strong woman your father raised. There isn't anything you can't do, Odette." She places her hand on my chest. "He lives here." Then, she moves her hand to my head. "And here. He will never leave you."

I pull her close. "Thank you, Florence. I don't know what I would do without you."

"I love you, Odette."

"Love you too."

Unknown: Odette. This is starting to get on my nerves. The more you ignore me every day, the more you push me to the extreme. Answer me!

Unknown: I'm afraid I will have to move forward with my plan. I'll see you soon love.

I can't keep this up. I haven't told the guys that *Unknown* has been getting more aggressive with his messages. I don't want to leave my dorm, fearing that he will do something to me. The guys think I'm going through depression, and if that's what I have to agree to, I will. They can't know what is going on.

"Jinx, we need to get going. You can't miss any more classes." Ashton stands in the doorway of my bedroom, eating an apple.

"Why? What's gonna happen?" I raise a questioning eyebrow.

He points his apple at me and grins. "You being the owner has its advantages, but you still need to get that little ass of yours into class."

"Fine, only because it'll do me good and not because you want me to go."

He chuckles. "Whatever you need to tell yourself. Oh, and you have a little visitor."

A little visitor?

"Edgar came back?"

He shrugs. That fucker. I race out of the room and see Atticus holding a black raven.

"Edgar, you finally came back. Where were you, buddy?" I reach out for him, and he turns his head, looking for a treat. "Hold on." Go figure the first thing he wants from me is food. Nothing has changed. I missed this little asshole.

"Kraa."

"Hold your fuckin' horses." I give Atticus the treat and watch Edgar swallow it whole. "Such a pig."

He flies over to me, landing at my feet. Kneeling in front of him, I pet under his beak. I missed my friend so much, and I wondered what adventures he went on; hopefully, he went someplace lovely. He nuzzles his head into my hand.

"I missed you."

"Kraa."

"One more treat, and then you can go."

"Kraa." He hops away, flying to the counter. He's like a dog getting excited over the word treat. Once he eats his last treat, he doesn't waste any time leaving. I watch him fly away, going wherever he goes. Lucky bastard.

"Baby, we should get going." Maddox says, holding up my bag.

I know it's time, but going out there where *Unknown* is doesn't sit well with me. What plan does he have for me? Maybe I should've written back to him and told him to leave the school and that I knew who he was.

Maddox digs in my bag, taking my phone out. "Your phone buzzed. It's probably Spence. Do you want me to read it to you?"

Before I could answer, he checked my phone.

His head whipped around unnaturally fast. "The fuck is this shit, Jinx?"

I went to answer, and Ashton snatched the phone from Maddox.

Ashton's mouth twitched in a snarl. "Jesus Christ, Jinx."

"Read it out loud, Ash," Atticus's voice turned dark.

I'm praying it's from Spencer. Please let it be from Spence.

Unknown: I know where your father's heart is.

TO BE CONTINUED...

ALSO BY

__A HITMAN'S DUET__
MYLES
CARTER

__RUSSO MAFIA SERIES__
UNBROKEN
UNBEARABLE
UNDENIABLE

__STRANGERS OF EASTWOOD__
STRANGERS OF THE NIGHT
STRANGERS OF THE TOWN
STRANGERS OF THE CROWD

__RAVENWOOD ACADEMY__
ATTICUS
ASHTON

__STANDALONE__
CHRISTMAS UNWRAPPED

__PAINFULLY OURS__
PAINFULLY MERRY

About the Author

Hello, loves! I'm a Canadian romance writer who's all about the steamy and dark stuff. Horror books, movies, and music? Yes, please! I have a little true crime obsession, but I'll just call it research and pretend it's normal.
If you crave love stories that push the limits of lust, trust, and desire, you've come to the right place.

Follow me for exclusive sneak peeks, giveaways, and behind-the-scenes glimpses into my writing process. And if you want to keep up with my latest releases or connect on social media.

Let's dive into the shadows together, darlings.

9 781999 891008 3